KT-457-977

TIPPING
THE WAITRESS
WITH DIAMONDS

TIPPING THE WAITRESS WITH DIAMONDS

BY

NINA HARRINGTON

MILLS & BOON®

All the characters in this book have no existence
outside the imagination of the author, and have
no relation whatsoever to anyone bearing the same
name or names. They are not even distantly inspired
by any individual known or unknown to the author,
and all the incidents are pure invention.

All Rights Reserved including the right of
reproduction in whole or in part in any form.
This edition is published by arrangement with
Harlequin Enterprises II BV/S.à.r.l. The text of this
publication or any part thereof may not be reproduced
or transmitted in any form or by any means, electronic
or mechanical, including photocopying, recording,
storage in an information retrieval system, or otherwise,
without the written permission of the publisher.

® and TM are trademarks owned and used by the
trademark owner and/or its licensee. Trademarks
marked with ® are registered with the United Kingdom
Patent Office and/or the Office for Harmonisation in
the Internal Market and in other countries.

First published in Great Britain 2010
Large Print edition 2010
Harlequin Mills & Boon Limited,
Eton House, 18-24 Paradise Road,
Richmond, Surrey TW9 1SR

© Nina Harrington 2010

ISBN: 978 0 263 21251 8

Harlequin Mills & Boon policy is to use papers that are
natural, renewable and recyclable products and made
from wood grown in sustainable forests. The logging and
manufacturing process conform to the legal environmental
regulations of the country of origin.

Printed and bound in Great Britain
by CPI Antony Rowe, Chippenham, Wiltshire

LONDON BOROUGH OF WANDSWORTH

9030 00001 1554 9	
Askews	23-Sep-2010
AF HARR	£13.99

SPECIAL RECIPE FOR THE PERFECT ROMANCE:

STEP 1
Take One Single Italian Girl

STEP 2
Add One Handsome Chef in a Kilt

STEP 3
Throw in Two Teaspoons of Shock and Uncertainty

STEP 4
Whisk Everything Together in a Tiny Bistro

STEP 5
Add a Couple of Big Decisions…

STEP 6
A Valentine Wish…

STEP 7
Two Sparkling Brown Eyes…

STEP 8
And a Pair of Pink Pyjamas

STEP 9
Sprinkle with Pink Flamingos

STEP 10
Add Hot Pink Psychedelic Flowers

STEP 11
And a Box of Warm Memories

STEP 12
Add a Platter of Sweet Dreams

STEP 13
And Three Wedding Cakes...

STEP 14
Eight Spinning Designer Rainbow Pizzas...

STEP 15
And Two Glasses of Red Wine

STEP 16
Smother in Wild Mushroom and Cream Sauce

STEP 17
Mix with Three Heaped Spoonfuls of Tears

STEP 18
And Two Pink Cupcakes

STEP 19
Add One American Chef Without a Kilt

STEP 20
Beat Vigorously

STEP 21
Finish with One Portion of Chocolate Tiramisu

STEP 22
Keep the Mixture Warm Until Valentine's Day; Top with a Red Rose Before Serving with a Kiss.

CHAPTER ONE

Step 1: Take One Single Italian Girl

ONCE UPON A time, Sienna Rossi thought as she sat back in a creaky staffroom chair, *restaurants were filled with wonderful guests who loved your food and drink and smiled sweetly to the waiting staff.*

Then she grimaced at the memory of the businessman who had snapped his fingers at her not once but *twice* within ten minutes, because first there had been too much ice in his drink and then his starter had arrived with a garnish of salad leaves which had clearly been added specifically to poison him. No leaves. *Those days were gone.*

I could have decorated the shoulders of his expensive business suit with the salad leaves and poured the dressing over his shiny head, Sienna thought.

But she wouldn't have done it, of course.

There was far too little dressing on the salad to

do any serious damage. Also, successful head waiters did not do things like that in exclusive country house hotels—especially head waiters who wanted desperately to be promoted to restaurant managers.

Now, if he had ordered Chef André's signature Hollandaise sauce... That might have been a different story.

Sienna yawned widely before reaching down to pull off her stylish high-heeled shoes and massaging her feet with a satisfied sigh of relief. She should be used to swollen hot feet and crushed toes after ten years in the restaurant trade but it never got easier—especially in luxury hotels which excelled in fine dining.

Greystone Manor had become famous for fabulous food and its glorious English country house setting, and business lunches were booked weeks in advance. She should be delighted that they had a full house every lunch and dinner service. Only it was *her* job, as head waiter and sommelier, to make sure that every single one of the sixty diners enjoyed some of the best food and wine in England, excellent service, and came away feeling that they had shared in the aristocratic lifestyle that living in a stately home could bring.

Unashamed award-winning luxury was tricky to pull off day after day.

It was like being an actress in a top London show, who had signed up to perform at both the matinee and the evening performances six days a week. In full make-up and tight costume, combined with even less comfortable shoes.

Singing and dancing on tables optional.

Sienna glanced at the huge antique wall clock as she rubbed the life back into her toes. Fifteen minutes to go. The new management team had called a special meeting to announce who they had decided to appoint to two crucial posts in their award-winning restaurant.

In a few minutes she would know the name of the new head chef. *And* find out who was going to be the restaurant manager who would be running front of house. That magical combination of wonderful food and excellent service which would take the Manor to the very top!

A shiver of anxiety ran across her shoulders and down her back, and she quickly checked that the staffroom was still empty. Of course she was nervous. But nobody else could know how scared she truly was.

Scared? Who was she kidding? Make that terrified.

On the glossy surface she was 'Miss Rossi'. The elegant and professional head waiter who was always immaculately turned out and who presented the perfect formal image the Manor aspired to in their fine-dining restaurant.

They would probably be horrified and totally amazed to know that the real Sienna Rossi was quaking inside the designer suit and shoes.

It had taken her four years of hard work to rebuild her shattered confidence to the point where she could even *think* about applying for the role of restaurant manager, in which she would be responsible for running her own projects and team.

This was going to be her dream job.

After so much sacrifice and hard work it was time to prove that she was capable of coming through heartbreak and rebuilding a career for herself.

A career in which she would never have to trust and rely on another person to make her dreams come true.

She *needed* this job so badly.

'You were a total star today. Did anyone tell you that? If I had an Oscar I would hand it over in an instant!'

Sienna blinked up from her reverie as her best

friend Carla burst through the swing doors with a characteristic gush of black suited hotel receptionist elegance and single city-girl attitude.

'Thanks. You're cutting it fine today,' Sienna replied with a smile. 'I thought the staff meeting was at four.'

Carla grabbed what was left of Sienna's coffee and swigged it down in one gulp before sighing out loud as the espresso cup hit the saucer.

'It is. Two of the guests managed to get lost in the maze. I know, I know.' Carla waved both hands in the air. 'That is supposed to be the point of having a proper maze in the first place. But in February? I'm freezing! It has taken me twenty minutes, using cellphones and a whistle, but they are now sitting all comfy and warm by the fire with hot tea and crumpets. *Unlike* the rest of us.'

Carla shivered inside her smart suit and shoved her hands deep under her armpits as Sienna poured her a fresh hot coffee.

'"Chefs in Kilts"!' Carla suddenly squealed, reaching forward to snatch up the colour supplement of the *Hotel Catering* magazine. 'Why didn't you tell me? I've been waiting all week for this! Who have they got as Hunk of the Month this time? Maybe we'll be working with one of these hot young celebrity chefs in a few weeks. Wouldn't that be totally cool?'

Not if I have anything to do with it, we won't, Sienna thought in silence. *Never again! Been there and do not want to go back, even for a visit. And it would not be cool.*

Carla shook her head before passing Sienna her precious magazine. 'See you in five minutes. And best of luck with the job, sweetie—not that you need it. Every confidence!' And with a small finger wave she was gone.

Sienna chuckled and started gathering together the coffee cups, but as she did so the magazine flipped open and the breath froze in her lungs at the sight of a studio photograph of a tall, muscular man in a white T-shirt and tartan kilt.

Hunk of the Month: Brett Cameron.

In an instant she was transported back twelve years, to the cramped and crowded kitchen of Trattoria Rossi. And her first passing glimpse of Aunt Maria's new trainee chef.

She'd been sixteen and had wandered straight from school into the kitchen, where her father and older brother, Frankie, had been prepping for the evening service. Training places at Rossi's were fought over at the catering college, and only the best students made the grade.

Dominating the kitchen had been a skinny teenager with fire in his eyes who'd had the cheek to argue with her brother, Frankie, over the best way to divide fresh basil.

And she had been smitten.

Completely. Absolutely. Without hesitation or rational thought.

Smitten.

Just one look. That was all it took.

She closed her eyes and revisited the vivid image that had been burnt into her memory all of those years ago.

Under a striped bandana, his long blond hair had been tied back in a ponytail which had highlighted the hard lines of a face so intense with suppressed fire and energy it that seemed to vibrate out and fill the air around him.

Every ounce of his concentration had been focused on the fresh green basil leaves in front of him, which he was tearing with long delicate fingers, while Frankie had shredded more fragrant leaves with a curved blade into thin strips.

Each of them had sprinkled sea salt and a little extra virgin olive oil onto their own stack of basil.

She had watched, entranced, as Frankie and then the blond had tasted each of the leaves in turn, with bread, then cheese and plum tomatoes, going back and forth between the two chopping boards until the blond had smiled up at Frankie and nodded.

Her brother had slapped the blond on the shoulder—which she had never seen him do to another chef in his life—and they'd turned around, smiling, to face her.

And for just one fraction of a second the skinny teenager had glanced up in her direction with such power and intense focus that it had felt as if a pair of pale blue lasers were boring holes through her skull.

Oh, boy...

Of course Frankie had broken off from the work to introduce his little sister to their new trainee, Brett, but by then she'd been a gibbering wreck.

No wonder he had responded to her squeaky hello with a low grunt. To Brett she must have seemed like just another idiot teenage girl—an interloper in this special world of edible sorcery where chefs were the magicians.

The fact that she'd been plump, awkward, clumsy and painfully shy when boys were around probably hadn't helped much, either.

For the next six weeks, which Brett had spent

learning the trade in the Trattoria Rossi kitchen, it had been amazing how many excuses Sienna had found to be in the kitchen at the same time.

Desperate for the chance to be close to Brett for a few seconds.

To smell him.

To feel the frisson of energy that seemed to spark in the very air around him as he worked feverishly. To hear his voice respond with 'Chef!' when her father passed an order for a salad or cold starter.

To run to the dining table on Sunday afternoons so that she could have the chair facing Brett at the family and crew communal meals.

No other boy at school or in her life had come close to the great Brett Cameron.

She had spent her schooldays in a dreamy daze, in anticipation of those precious few moments when she could see him again, in the evening and at weekends.

Even if she *had* been so shy back then that she'd been totally incapable of speaking to him. That would have been far too terrifying even to consider.

Brett Cameron had been her first crush.

For a fleeting second Sienna succumbed to a ripple of those same teenage fears and intense shyness. She wasn't the first schoolgirl who had ever felt like a total outsider and fraud, and no doubt she would not be the last, but merely thinking back to those sad days was enough to take her to a dark place.

She shook off the memory and blinked hard to clear her head.

They had both come a long way since then.

Sienna smiled down at the magazine article and chuckled to herself for the first time that day. Hunk of the Month, indeed!

He was still the best-looking chef she had ever seen!

Back then, the nineteen-year-old Brett had been a tall, skinny teenager with a total obsession for food. His only clothing had been chef's trousers and two identical off-white T-shirts that had become increasingly less fragrant as each week went on.

Now he looked as if a team of professional stylists had spent hours working on him. And it had been money well spent for one of the top chefs now taking the catering world by storm. Last time she had seen his name in the press he had been accepting an award for a hotel restaurant in Australia. That probably explained the suntan which made those blue eyes sparkle even brighter.

He certainly had filled out. The white shirt

stretched out across wide shoulders below a firm neck and a solid jawline defined by expertly clipped short blond hair.

Two things had not changed.

His eyes were still winter-sea-blue. Smiling out at her.

Sharp. Intelligent. Focused.

Tiny white smile lines fanned out from the corners of his tanned face. Well, he certainly had plenty to smile about. He had come a long way from Maria Rossi's tiny trattoria in North London to headline in the Food and Drink Awards 'Top New Chef' list.

And then there were his hands. In this photograph they were splayed out on each hip. Those clever fingers, which had used to move so fast that she'd been afraid to blink in case she missed something crucial. Long narrow fingers. How many hours had she spent dreaming about those hands?

She had fallen for those hands. No doubt about it. The only other man who had come close to having hands like those was Angelo.

Oh, Brett. If you only knew the trouble you have caused me!

She blamed him entirely for giving her a chef addiction virus. That well known form of contagion and pestilence.

At college, Carla had given her the nickname of 'chef magnet'.

Any chef within a hundred-mile radius would somehow sense that Sienna was within range and hit on her.

The chiming of the clock snapped Sienna out of her dreamy thoughts, and she glanced at the photo for one last time before closing the magazine and squeezing her swollen feet back into her shoes.

Drat! She was going to be late!

One more thing to blame on Brett Cameron! Wherever in the world he might be!

She need not have rushed! Sienna had been sitting very impatiently with the rest of the hotel management team for almost ten minutes before Patrick breezed into the dining room with head chef André following a few steps behind.

Patrick was the stylish hotel manager for the company who owned the Manor and a small group of other luxury hotels in the most prestigious locations across Europe—hotels where Sienna had every intention of working as a top restaurant manager. *After* she'd persuaded them to give her the position of restaurant manager here at Greystone Manor, of course.

She wanted this job *so* badly. It was everything she had been working towards since the first time she'd put on a waitress uniform in the Rossi family restaurant back in London.

Little wonder that her heart was racing.

Patrick looked around the room and smiled as he tapped gently on a water glass with a table knife. A sense of anxious anticipation ran around the room as the nervous chatter fell away.

'Thank you all for coming at such short notice. As you know, our brilliant head chef André Michon will be retiring at the end of the month, after thirty-two years of amazing work at the Manor. I'm already looking forward to his retirement party, but in the meantime André's decision has given the management team a real headache. How can we possibly find another chef with the same passion for excellence and quality that has made the Manor so successful?'

Please just get on with it, Sienna thought, bristling with impatience. *Please tell me who I will be working with from next month!*

'I am delighted to tell you that we have interviewed some of the brightest young chefs in the world over these last few months, and after much deliberation there was one clear winner. Ladies and gentlemen, I am very pleased to announce that the new head chef at Greystone Manor will be…TV celebrity chef Angelo Peruzi! I know that you must all be thrilled as I am.'

Sienna clutched hold of the sides of her chair with both hands and sucked in several breaths to keep herself from falling over or running out of the room in horror.

No. No. No. Not Angelo.

No. Fate would not play tricks like that on her. It had to be some sort of mistake. She could not have just heard that name.

Sienna sat frozen, her brain stunned. Exploding in on itself with the implications. And the horror.

Her heart was racing so fast and hard that it frightened her, and she fought not to burst into tears or scream out loud.

Angelo! Of all the chefs in the entire world they had to choose the one man who she wanted nothing to do with again. Her ex-fiancé. The man who had abandoned her a month before their wedding to heartbreak and despair.

This could not be happening. Not now. Not to her. Not here. Not after four years.

No! Hot tears pricked the corners of her eyes, blinding her to what was going on around her.

It took a few seconds for her to acknowledge that Carla was prodding her in the arm and gesturing with her head towards the dais. Patrick was saying something about a new restaurant manager.

'Miss Sienna Rossi has already shown what she can achieve as head waiter. Welcome to the team and many congratulations, Miss Rossi. I know that you will make a terrific restaurant manager. Chef Peruzi simply can't wait to start working with you!'

CHAPTER TWO

Step 2: Add One Handsome Chef in a Kilt

BRETT CAMERON stood with both hands thrust deep inside the pockets of his cargo trousers and stared up at the rubble-strewn building site that was destined to become his first signature restaurant.

Just four days earlier he had been in sunny Adelaide, celebrating at his leaving party, turning steaks on a barbecue and looking forward to working in his own kitchen in central London.

The reality of a wet, grey February afternoon, with deafening London traffic on the other side of this gate, was not quite the warm and glamorous welcome he might have liked, but at that moment he was totally oblivious to the noise and heavy drizzle.

This was it. After years of dreaming and planning it was finally going to happen. And from all of the possible locations in the world he had to choose from there was only one city he wanted to come back to.

It had to be London.

This was the city where he had suffered the worst years of his life as an angry and frustrated teenager, coming to terms with what life had thrown at him.

Back then London had been just one more cold and unfriendly place, where his single mother had dragged him from one cheap rented apartment to another while she found two or sometimes three unskilled jobs in order to pay the rent and keep their heads above water.

Jobs in which you did not need to read or write very well to earn a wage.

The kind of jobs he had come to detest—and yet he had been clever enough to recognise them as the kind of work he would probably find himself doing from the moment he was old enough to leave school.

Who wanted to employ a boy who could barely write his name and address on an application form, even assuming that he could read the questions in the first place?

A boy whom every one of the ten or more schools he had attended had labelled as having 'behavioural difficulties'? No matter how hard he'd worked and worked it had made no difference to the stigma of being classified as slow or lazy. An academic failure.

If he was going to prove to the world just how very far that boy had come, and what he had achieved in the years since he'd last walked these streets, then he had to come back to London.

Brett inhaled the moist air.

No regrets. It wasn't all bad. His life as a chef had begun in this city.

It was hard to believe that Maria Rossi's restaurant and his old catering college were only a few miles down the road! Sometimes it felt like a lifetime ago. A lifetime of exhaustion, hard work and even harder experience.

Maria Rossi hadn't known for sure what she was taking on all those years ago, when she'd given him a chance.

She had taken a huge risk with a stranger, not knowing how he was going to turn out, but had faith enough to make the commitment anyway.

Just as he was doing here.

There might be banks and financiers willing enough to back his new restaurant, but this was still totally personal. His own kitchen.

In a world where even successful restaurants struggled to make a living, it was precisely the kind of crazy, exciting, thrilling project he couldn't wait to get started on.

Energy coursed through his veins. *This was the greatest adventure of his life!*

Even the physical reality of bricks and mortar was exhilarating. Until now this place had just been an idea. A dream he had talked about with his friend Chris over endless cups of coffee and glasses of wine in the two hectic years they had spent in Paris as students almost a decade ago.

And now he was looking at that dream brought to life.

He had barely slept on the long flight from Australia. His mind had been a buzz of menus and all the bewildering and complex combinations of who and what and where that went into creating a successful restaurant business.

'Where's your kilt today, old chap?' A powerful well-spoken English voice boomed out from the well-spoken, short, stout man who came striding up to Brett between stacks of bricks. 'Left it back in Oz?'

Brett grasped hold of his best friend's hand, then reached back and gave him a slap on the back.

'Don't you start!' Brett replied, in an accent tinged with an Australian twang. 'Brilliant publicity, as always, but you *do* know that I only spent the first two months of my life in Glasgow? I'm never going to live that down in the Cameron clan!'

'I'm sure they'll get over it when this palace of modern cuisine is opened! What do you think of the progress so far?' Chris nodded towards the building site just as a length of waste timber came flying out of a side window and crashed to the tarmac below, to join a mound of broken bricks and wood.

Brett grinned at the fragments of timber and nodded a few times with pursed lips before replying.

'It's good to see people with so much enthusiasm for their work! I'll answer that question after you've shown me the kitchen!' Brett rubbed both his hands together and his mouth lifted into a broad grin of delight. 'I have been looking forward to this for a long time.'

Chris straightened a little, lifted his head, and gritted his teeth together in a sharp hiss.

'Ah. About the kitchen. Slight delay, I'm afraid. Not *quite* ready for inspection yet.' As Brett turned to look at him, Chris gestured with his head towards a huge mound of tarpaulin-covered shapes just inside the main entrance.

Brett swallowed down hard in silence, took a breath, and strode into what would be the main reception area once the walls had been finished. His shoulders were high with tension.

He carefully and gingerly lifted up one of the tarpaulins and stared in silence at the huge packaging crates.

'Tell me that's not what I think it is!' Brett blurted out, his voice a mix of barely concealed horror and amazement.

'Afraid so,' Chris replied with a tilt of his head. 'The ovens were held up in transit. Apparently cargo ships don't like to go out in hurricane-force winds. Winter. Ocean. Big waves. Tricky things. Strange, that, isn't it?'

Brett stared awestruck at the huge pile of boxes and containers and raked his hands through his hair, before turning back to the only person who truly understood the sacrifices he had made to arrive at this point, when his restaurant was so close to becoming a reality.

Chris shrugged back at him. 'Can't do anything until the ovens are fitted and tested. You know that. Your dream kitchen is going to be full of brick dust and filth for at least a couple of days. You wanted the best and you're going to have the best. Only not this week. Maybe longer.'

Chris faltered and raised both hands in the air as Brett groaned in reply and closed his eyes.

'I know,' Chris acknowledged. 'I've already used up all of the slack we planned on the building work. It's going to be tough to make the deadline.'

'Make that *very* tough,' Brett answered with a nod. 'We only have a couple of weeks before the doors open to paying customers, and I still don't have menus or staff. This building needs to be finished as soon as we can, or we could be late on the first payment of the bank loan. And our credibility will suffer.'

His fingers worked through his hair behind each ear. 'Maybe it wasn't such a good idea to invite all the key London food critics and journalists to our opening night when we hadn't started the building work yet?'

'It was great idea!' Chris replied. 'This is why I've set up a meeting with the architects, so we can bring you up to date on the project plan. You're the only one who can decide what compromises you are willing to make to push the project through. They'll be expecting us in about an hour.'

'An hour?' Brett chortled and gave a shake of his head. 'In that case you had better start talking me though the plan. Let's start with the services and—' The sound of an Italian tenor rang out loud from Brett's cellphone. He glanced at the caller ID, and then looked at it more closely before nodding to Chris.

'Sorry, mate. Have to take this one. Be with you in a minute.'

'No problem. Let me get that snag list.'

Brett flicked open the phone as Chris strolled away through the debris, and grinned to himself before answering the call.

'Maria Rossi's galley slave, here. Ready to do your bidding, oh, great one!'

Only instead of Maria Rossi's, a man's voice bellowed down the line.

'Hello? Is that Brett? Brett Cameron?'

'Yes. This is Brett Cameron. Can you I help you?' he replied, holding the phone away from his ear to prevent damage to his hearing.

'Oh, good. This is Henry. You know—Maria Rossi's friend from the ballroom-dancing class. I'm calling from *Spain*. She asked me to call you.'

Henry? Had he ever met a Henry? Maria had so many friends it was hard to keep up.

'Hi, Henry. Is everything okay?'

'No. Sorry, but Maria's in the hospital. Oh, don't worry. She's going to be fine. Are you there? Brett?'

The smile fell from Brett's face and he inhaled sharply before replying.

'Yes—yes, I'm still here. What happened? Has there been an accident? Is she hurt?'

'No, no, nothing like that. Did Maria tell you that she was going on the dance club trip to Benidorm? That's here in Spain, you know.'

'She didn't mention it, but, yes, I understand. What's happened to Maria, Henry?'

'Well. I don't really know. She was on her way back from the banana boat race yesterday afternoon when the pain started. At first we blamed too much paella and sangria in the club last night, but a few hours later she slumped over in the Spanish dancing class. Right in the middle of the Paso Doble. They carted her off to the local hospital. The instructor carried her to the ambulance. It was very exciting.'

'Exciting? Right. Did they say what's wrong with her?'

'Appendicitis. Caught just in time. Nasty, that. That's why I'm phoning, see. To tell you that she *is* okay. Surgery was fine but she's going to be here for at least— Oh, here she is. I need to pretend to be injured now.'

There was a shuffle, and the sound of fierce whispering on the other end of the line before a familiar and surprisingly cheerful voice sounded in his ear.

'Hello, Chef Cameron. Are you back?'

Brett smiled gently. The irrepressible Maria Rossi! Not even major surgery could hold this lady back for long!

'I am, boss. But never mind about me. What's all this about you being in hospital? Charming the handsome young doctors in Spain?'

A faint female voice laughed in reply. 'I've been kidnapped! One small operation and they want to keep me tied to this bed for two weeks! They even tried to confiscate my cellphone! I've had to crawl out onto the fire escape while Henry distracts them for a few minutes with a paper cut on his thumb.'

'Well, resist the temptation to make your daring escape. You can't fool me, Maria Rossi. There are probably teams of medical staff waiting on your every need. Now for the really important questions: what's the food like, and how are you feeling? And do not try and fob me off. Appendicitis can be serious!'

'The operation went fine, no complications—
and I've had worse meals. But I'm knackered.
Woman in the next bed snored the whole night.
Did not get a wink of sleep.' Maria took a breath
before asking, 'Have you got a fast car?'

'I can find one. Want me to drive down to the
Costa Brava and pick you up?'

'Don't tempt me with offers like that! Thanks,
but I do need a favour. Would you mind heading
over to my place to make sure Rossi's is still
standing? Sienna won't be able to manage without
someone to do the cooking for her.'

'Sienna? Is that the new trainee chef you're ter-
rorising in my place?'

'Sienna Rossi. My *niece*. Frank's sister. You
probably don't remember her. Anyway, the poor
girl left me a couple of voice messages earlier to
tell me she was on her way over to Rossi's to stay
with me for a few days. She sounded distressed,
but by the time I could call her back her phone was
turned off. Sienna doesn't know I'm away. I don't
like the idea of her turning up to find me gone and
the place closed up.'

Then Maria chuckled to herself. 'I love that girl
dearly, but there is no telling what she could get
up to if she is left in charge of Rossi's for two

weeks. She'll probably be running herself ragged trying to open up the place on her own.'

Brett snorted in reply. 'I wonder who that reminds me of? Chip off the old block, there. Why don't you just close the place for an extra week or two?'

There was a long pause on the other end of the line.

'Maria? Still there? Or have the nurses dragged you back inside?'

'Oh, still here—but I can't talk for long. Look, Brett. I won't beat around the bush. Things are not going too well at the moment and I need the business. To be honest, I can't afford to close down for another two weeks. Be a good lad and promise me you'll lend a hand?' She paused. 'It would help put my mind at rest if I knew that you could keep the old place going, rake in some cash, and look after Sienna for me.'

'Okay. It's a promise. I'll head over there tonight.'

Maria sighed in relief. 'You're a star. I should warn you that— Oops! I've been spotted. Later.'

And with that she was gone, to the sound of shuffles and muffled voices, before the call clicked off, leaving a stunned Brett in the bustle of electric drills and workmen.

Maria was obviously recovering well, but there had been no mistaking the concern in her voice.

February was always a slow month in the restaurant trade. And many of her regular customers were elderly couples who had been going there for years. Cold winter evenings and tight budgets… Hmm, that could mean trouble for any small restaurant.

Small? Who was he kidding? Maria's dining room was about the same size as the new reception area in the building he was looking at now.

Brett flicked down the cover on his cellphone. He owed Maria Rossi everything. This remarkable woman had taken a chance with a troubled teenager whom the world had labelled an academic failure. Over the years he had made it his business to keep in touch with her. Let her know how he was doing.

It was Maria Rossi who had stood by his side at the Young Chef of the Year Awards.

Maria Rossi who had opened the door to the most prestigious restaurants in Paris, where he'd learnt the true meaning of fine cooking.

And Maria Rossi who had persuaded the catering college to run a test which proved that he was not slow, not stupid, and certainly not lazy.

He had dyslexia.

And now he was back in London for the first time in ten years with something to prove, and Maria wanted him to do her a favour.

Consider it done.

As for Sienna Rossi? Oh, he remembered Sienna Rossi. He remembered Miss Sienna Rossi very well indeed.

'Everything okay? You look very thoughtful!'

Brett looked around to find Chris staring at him in concern, a large bundle of papers scrunched under one arm.

The architects!

'Sorry, mate. Change of plan. I have to help out an old friend for a few days. You're going to have to take the meeting on your own. I know you can handle it. Call me whenever you need me, but I have to go.'

CHAPTER THREE

Step 3: Throw in Two Teaspoons of Shock and Uncertainty

IT WAS almost seven in the evening when Sienna stepped gingerly down from the red London bus and shrugged herself deeper into her raincoat. The drizzle had been replaced by light rain, and the air was moist and heavy with diesel fumes and the city smog of a dark winter evening.

For the first week in February there was still a definite snap of cold in the air, and Sienna regretted her decision to leave Greystone Manor without changing into winter shoes, but it all happened in such a rush!

It had been surprisingly easy to convince Patrick that she needed to take the two weeks' holiday she was owed before the new chef arrived and she started work on their 'exciting new project'!

Pity that she was still as confused and undecided as she had been a few hours earlier. The shakes might have eased off, but she knew better. Shock and awe did not even come close! The train journey from Greystone had been a nightmare: sharing a carriage with happy people on their way to enjoy an evening show in London when all she had wanted to do was curl up into a small ball and whimper.

At least her legs were a little steadier. She had almost fainted in the dining room when Patrick had announced Angelo's name. It was lucky for her that everyone had been too busy to hang around and chat about the announcement, and she'd been able to escape to the sanctuary of her bedroom on wobbly legs.

She sucked in a deep breath of cool night air and blinked hard to clear her head as hot burning tears again pricked her eyes and seared her dry throat.

No tears. You are not going to cry, she told herself sternly.

She had done more than enough crying over Angelo Peruzi!

And now he had come back to Britain. To her home. To her safe place.

Sienna sensed her fists clench and unclench, the knuckles white, as she took another deep breath. She was a professional. She was used to handling problems. She could handle this one just like the others.

Focus on the options.

Basically she had two choices. Stay. Or go.

She could stay and be professional and keep her home by agreeing to work with Angelo and take the restaurant to the next level. They would be colleagues. Professionals working together. Nothing more. This could be the chance she had been waiting for to show what she could do on the international scene and persuade the hotel chain to transfer her to another restaurant.

Or—and this second option was so terrible that she mentally braced herself even to think about it—she could leave and start again somewhere else.

She would have to give up the job she loved and…and do what? Ask for a transfer? That was a possibility. She could always find another job as a head waiter, but it would probably set her back a year or two while she rebuilt her team.

Or she could run back to the Rossi clan with her tail between her legs. Her parents might have retired, but her brother, Frankie, was running an Italian delicatessen with his young wife and family—maybe she could ask them for a job?

And throw away four years of very hard work in the process.

No. She couldn't bear to think about that.

One thing was certain. She had to think this through. And fast. Angelo would be at the Manor in less than a week. She needed her parents—except they had chosen the perfect time to take in a cruise. And she wasn't even sure that they could help her.

That left the only person she could rely on for advice. Her aunt Maria Rossi.

Rubbing her arms for warmth, Sienna turned the corner and was immediately struck by the illuminated signs from not one but two pizza and noodle shops flashing in the dusky gloom. A lot had changed in the six months since her last short visit to this part of London.

Sienna paused on the pavement so that she could look across the narrow street at Rossi's, as it had always been known. This was where her aunt had offered her refuge from the disaster that had been Angelo Peruzi. Ironic that the same man was driving her back here now. She needed a warm hug, a hot meal, and all the advice that Maria could give. *And she needed them desperately!*

Under the streetlights there was no escaping the fact that there were a few more things that had certainly changed over the winter months—and not for the better.

Maria had some serious competition here!

Trattoria Rossi stood in what had been a prime location, set back slightly from the main street with just enough space out front for two or three patio tables. Except this was February, and the rain had a definite touch of sleet in it.

The harsh fluorescent light seemed to highlight the fact that the paint was peeling badly from the hand-painted sign that had once proudly carried the words *TRATTORIA ROSSI*. Several letters had faded to the point where to a passing car the sign might seem to be spelling out *RATT…OS*.

But that was not the worst of it. As Sienna skipped across the road at the crossing, the first thing she saw as she approached the bistro was a large crack in the plate-glass front window. Cracks in one corner spread out like a spider's web, sideways into the glass.

Standing in front of the bistro at that moment, Sienna struggled to recall what it had looked like when she had last visited Maria in daylight—sparkling clean, bright and cheerful. A welcoming and friendly family bistro—an ideal place to spend a lunchtime. What she was looking at now was dismal and dark and the kind of place she would never choose to eat. Even if it was open.

Which it wasn't.

A handwritten sign said—as best as she could read in the dim light and poor handwriting—that the restaurant was closed due to staff holiday and would be open again for lunch next week. Only which week and when it had been written was not made clear.

Her family would have told her if Maria was on holiday. Wouldn't they?

Oh, Maria. Where are you when I need you?

Emotion flooded through Sienna. For a few seconds she allowed the stress of the day to overwhelm her, and she bent over from the waist and clasped hold of her knees with her eyes closed.

Please be here. Please! It was not much to ask! She simply needed someone to be here whom she could trust and take refuge in.

With a loud sniff, Sienna pushed herself back to her full height.

This was what falling for chefs did for you! Dratted Brett Cameron! Or Angelo. Or both!

Perhaps tonight was Maria's night out? The Nifty after Fifty dance club members were some of her best customers and Maria was no slouch when it came to showing her own skills in the ballroom.

Cupping her hands around her eyes and peering through the glass, Sienna was relieved to see that electric lights were on in the kitchen, and she could hear the thump-thump beat of pop music above the noise of the traffic which was whizzing past her.

Someone must be working there. Maria always had at least one trainee chef and a waitress working for her. Usually one of them lived with Maria in the cosy house connected to the trattoria. Only, the house was in complete darkness.

Sienna knocked hard on the front door of the trattoria just as the rain started to fall more heavily. She had planned to spend the night in Maria's house, and the keys were inside the bistro. It was time to either wake somebody up or start ringing doorbells along the street to find out if anyone else had a key. Maria was so trusting it would not surprise her if half the elderly neighbours had spares.

Except, of course, most of the ladies were probably with Maria at the their local ballroom-dancing class, while she stood there and stamped her feet to avoid being frozen to the spot.

After her third attempt at battering down the door, and then ringing the doorbell at Maria's house, Sienna decided that it was time to try plan B. The rear door to the kitchen.

It was at this point that the rain became a more intense sleet, which dripped from the tree branches and cascaded from the rooftops of the parade of shops onto the pavement below—and anyone who happened to be walking there, trying to find the gate behind the bistro. Stiff with rain and misuse, the old wooden gate stubbornly refused to open, and Sienna had to abandon her luggage to the wet yard which was slick with rain water and unknown slime, and use both hands to push hard and lift at the same time.

The gate gave way in a rush, so that she half fell, half stumbled headfirst into the yard and almost lost her footing. Taking a moment to calm her breathing, Sienna sighed in relief. Her reward was that Maria's kitchen was still brightly lit and definitely the source of the music.

Sliding her luggage forward, Sienna tiptoed as best she could between the rubbish bins, sodden cardboard boxes and discarded plastic trays towards the back door, trying to save her shoes from the puddles of rainwater which had filled the gaps between the broken cement slabs and mystery dark objects which blocked the path. Nothing scurried away, meowed or barked as she dodged the blockade, which was a real plus.

There was a vertical line of light beaming out from the back door—it was open!

Maria must be home!

Her shoulders relaxed in relief. Thank goodness.

There was no sign of anyone through the kitchen windows, but, undaunted, Sienna took a step closer to the gap in the heavy metal back door.

Only at that precise moment the door swung open wider. And in one flash of an eyelid Sienna Maria Rossi took in three startling facts.

Leaning forward in the doorway was a tall dark figure, whose face was in the shadow of the bright kitchen light.

Attached to one long forearm was a pink plastic bucket, in which something was sloshing loudly from side to side as the arm drew back.

The arm was bent back for a very good reason. The bucket was already moving forward in a graceful arc to be emptied into the backyard. Only she was in the way and there was nothing either of them could do about it.

Half a bucket of warm water hit Sienna straight in the legs, and she only just had enough time to squeeze her eyes shut before the deluge splashed up to her knees, narrowly missing the bottom of her suit skirt as the cascade flooded into the tops of both shoes, filling them with dirty water she did not even want to think about, as well as soaking her luggage.

There was a horrified gasp from the figure standing in the doorway followed by a rasp of deep male laughter.

Sienna squeezed her eyes tighter together. *This person—this man—*was actually laughing about the fact that he had just completely soaked her legs and ruined her best work shoes in the process. Goodness knew what state her luggage would be in.

This was a wretched end to a terrible, terrible day. *It could not possibly get any worse.*

She slowly, slowly opened her eyes and wiped away the rainwater with one hand, before lifting her head to face the enemy. Only she never got the chance—because before she knew what was happening a strong male arm had wrapped around her wet shoulders and half dragged, half supported her towards the door.

'Hi, Sienna. Sorry about that. It's great to see you again. Want to come inside and dry off?'

Sienna looked up, blinking against the bright kitchen light, and stared, open-mouthed in shock, into the face of the man who was lifting her bag from her sodden fingers. Then the blood rushed to her head so quickly that she felt dizzy and leaned back against the door frame to steady herself before she could trust her voice to say tremulously, *'Brett?'*

A tousle-haired blond with a wide smile touched two fingers to his brow in mock salute.

'Welcome back to Rossi's. It's going to be *just* like old times.'

And at that point the ever cool and in control Sienna Rossi burst into tears.

CHAPTER FOUR

Step 4: Whisk Everything Together in a Tiny Bistro

SILENT TEARS streamed down Sienna's face, blinding her to everything and everybody.

Shoulders heaving, she tried to control her sobs and snatch back some form of self-control in tiny breaths.

This was agony!

There was a lump in her throat the size of an egg, her eyes must be red and puffy, and goodness knows what her hair must look like! What a complete mess!

She had never felt so humiliated in her life!

This, of course, made her feel even more wretched!

There was no way she would ever be able to look Brett Cameron in the face again. Perhaps she could emigrate? To a distant planet?

Or perhaps she had simply imagined the whole thing and the rain and her tears had blurred her vision?

Then he spoke, in a low, caring voice, and her heart twisted.

'Here. Let me take that wet coat for you.'

Before she had time to argue the point Brett had moved behind her and was lifting her raincoat from her shoulders.

His fingertips gently grazed the sides of her throat for a fraction of a second, sending delicious shivers across her shoulders and down her arms. She immediately covered the shiver by rubbing the palms of her hands up and down the arms of the thin cashmere cardigan she had thrown over her silk blouse, as though it was the damp and cold that had made her body quiver rather than the simple touch of those clever fingers.

'You're freezing! Take this. I'm more than warm enough.'

A soft extra-large and very masculine fleece jacket was wrapped around her shoulders, and she sighed in delight and relief before shrugging her arms into the sleeves and pulling the zip high to the neck. She was practically sitting on the hem when she straightened her skirt and snuggled into the wonderful warm comfort. It was like wearing a quilt.

Heaven.

And it was infused with his own personal scent.

'Better?' he asked, looking into her face with concern, then rubbed his hands down the length of her arms, flushing her with glowing warmth—and not just from the soft fabric.

'Much,' she managed to reply with a brief nod, before noticing that he was now wearing only a cotton short-sleeved T-shirt. All the fight and bluff she had planned died on her quivering lips. 'Thank you.'

'How do you like your tea?' He reached behind him to the worktop and picked up a steaming hot drink. 'I take mine white with two sugars. Careful now.'

Brett hunkered down on the wet floor and pressed the hot beaker between her cold shaking fingers, waiting until her sobs subsided before helping her wrap her fingers tightly enough so that she would not spill it.

The look of concern and anxiety in those blue eyes almost started Sienna off again, so she swallowed down a large sip of hot tea, feeling the warmth spread from her throat, and then another sip, until she was holding the beaker on her own.

Only then did Brett push himself effortlessly back on his heels to his full height, his slender strong fingers slipping away from hers, breaking their tenuous connection.

Sienna swallowed down another swig of the welcome hot tea. Strange that she usually hated sweet tea with milk but at that moment it was the only thing she wanted.

The room seemed to come more into focus. She was sitting on a tiny metal patio chair that not even the local scamps would have stolen from the pavement in front of the bistro—they had *some* standards. She took a breath, squeezed her eyes shut, flicked them open, and did a double-take.

The lights were still on. She had shaken most of the rain from her hair and eyes. And it was definitely Brett Cameron or an identical twin brother she knew nothing about.

There was no mistaking the piercing blue eyes, and they were certainly the same hands which had touched her skin for the very first time only a few minutes earlier.

Too handsome to be true Brett Cameron.

Obsessive, passionate, serious, eyes as blue as the sea Brett Cameron.

The same Brett Cameron who had either totally ignored her or at best acknowledged her presence with a grunt or a nod for six complete weeks when he'd worked as a trainee chef, and then every Saturday evening when she'd worked here as a waitress for her aunt.

The same Brett Cameron who had haunted her schoolgirl dreams and was nowadays being photographed for catering magazines.

That Brett Cameron was at that very moment taking up most of the space in her aunt's kitchen.

And she was wearing his fleece and drinking his tea.

How had that happened?

It was as though the last ten years of her life had been an absurd dream, and she was back to being a gawky, awkward and awestruck sixteen year old.

Then he stretched forward to hoist her bag onto a bar stool and turn down the lively jazz music, and she got the full benefit of the well-worn grey rock-star T-shirt stretched over a broad chest and powerful shoulders.

The over thin, scrawny teenage version of Brett had been replaced by a man who looked as though he had spent his time in Australia on the beach. Or surfing. Those Chefs in Kilts photos had definitely not needed fancy editing!

Shame that those same teenage hormones now flared hot in her veins as a full-colour vision of a topless and tanned Brett in board shorts flashed in panoramic full-colour detail across her mind. Perhaps she had not changed as much as she thought she had?

Oh, no. *Not now.* Not on top of the news about Angelo. Two men. Both chefs. *Doomed.*

Sienna groaned softly to herself. This was starting to feel like a conspiracy.

'Sorry about your nice shoes! I should have paid more attention to the front doorbell.'

Well, that was new! The teenage Brett had used to have trouble saying even a few words over the Rossi dinner table—and then only when her aunt Maria had forced the words out of him. Now he was noticing her shoes!

Who was this man? And at what point in the last few years had he started to notice women's *footwear?*

She stared down at her sodden feet and squelched her cold wet toes inside what had once been designer couture heels. Now the leather felt positively slimy, and destined for the nearest wastebin. And at precisely that moment she realised that she had not packed any spare shoes in her rush to leave Greystone as fast as Carla had been able to drive her to the railway station.

No spare shoes. Not even a pair of slippers.

Her eyes closed and she quivered on the edge of more tears. Self-pity this time.

This was what happened when you dropped everything for chefs!

You left work wearing high heels with soles the thickness of writing paper.

In the rain.

In February.

The sensible and totally in-control version of Sienna Rossi who would have packed a range of suitable footwear to choose from had clearly left the building!

Hearing the name Angelo Peruzi being announced, after seeing gorgeous Brett Cameron in that magazine had clearly puddled her poor brain beyond rational thought. That was the only possible explanation for it. She would have to just sit there in wet shoes for the rest of the evening. Until she could escape to the shops to buy new ones or—gulp—borrow some of Aunt Maria's shoes. She had clear memories of her aunt's more memorable shoes. Bows. Stripes. *Flowers!*

Sienna lifted one foot and then the other out

of the standing water on the tiled floor and fixed her heels behind the lowest rung of the back of her patio chair as Brett moved a heavy bucket out of reach and swished an industrial sized absorbent sponge over the tiles below, where she had been standing.

'Thank you.' At this point the sensible part of her brain started to kick in with extra warmth. 'They *were* nice shoes.' She looked at the back of his tanned head and was distracted by the tight-cut dark blond layers above wide shoulders, strong biceps and toned forearm. 'I'm amazed to see you here, Brett! Last time I spoke to Maria you were in Australia! This has come as a bit of a surprise!'

He stopped mopping for a second and turned back towards her, flashing a killer smile she had imagined was the product of airbrushing for those magazine shots.

But this was the real thing. White, white teeth contrasted against tanned blond stubble around a wide mouth which turned up more on the right side than the left as he smiled.

To her absolute horror Sienna's treacherous stomach performed a full somersault and backflip that would have pleased an Olympic swimmer.

Oh, boy.

The Hunk of the Month photo did not come close to Brett Cameron up close and personal— even if he *was* wearing denims which had seen cleaner and dryer days.

How dared he be even more handsome than she remembered from of those years ago?

'You never did like surprises.' He smiled back at her. 'Some things clearly haven't changed.'

He leant back on the workbench and crossed his arms over his wide chest, dominating the space between them as though he owned the place and always had done. His focused gaze made Sienna want to squirm and deny the accusation, but she deflected it by raising her head higher and trying to look uninterested.

'Would you believe me if I told you that your aunt Maria offered me a job mopping up while she was away on holiday in Spain?' Brett continued. 'Hard to turn down an opportunity like that! How could I resist? Jumped on the first plane back to London!'

A muscle twitched in the right corner of his mouth to match the twinkle in his eyes.

He was teasing her.

She was soaked, cold, tired and miserable.

And her aunt Maria was away on holiday.

Suddenly she felt as though the whole world has deserted her. *Double doomed.*

And Brett Cameron was teasing her. Looking for a reaction. Well, she could play the game as well as he could. All she had to was persuade her brain to start working again while she ignored her damp, dirty legs and feet.

At least the kitchen was warm. Even though it was wet. Very wet. *Too* wet.

From her patio chair, the view over the tiny kitchen was of uniformly shiny and wet floor tiles, with deeper standing water in some of the corners.

Brett had not been cleaning the floor. He had been trying to soak up a major flood. At least that explained why he'd been emptying his bucket outside. And why his boots and trousers were dark and soaked through almost as far as the knees.

Strange how knowing that he was also enjoying the benefit of cold clothing against his legs made her feel a lot better. And now curiosity won the battle between her deciding to be indifferent to his suffering or finding out why one of the allegedly finest young chefs in the world was mopping kitchen floors.

'I can see how you wouldn't want to miss that kind of offer. As for the mopping up... Let me guess. Has there has been a flood? The chest freezer defrosted?'

Brett shifted position and tilted his head to one side. 'Close. According to the girl I found trying to cope, Maria doesn't have a big freezer any more. It sort of caught fire and was never replaced. In fact, you probably had to scramble over it to get to the back door. This—' and he gestured with his head to the far corner of the room where the water looked deeper '—was the dishwasher.'

Sienna looked at him for a second, wide eyed, before blowing out hard. Freezers did not catch fire at Greystone Manor.

'The big freezer caught fire? Right. Any idea what happened to the dishwasher? Was there a power failure?'

'I wish!' Brett replied with a snort. 'Oh, sorry. Actually, it's not funny. Apparently the ancient rust bucket had been leaking for weeks, but Maria never got around to having it fixed before her holiday. Julie came in to open up for you and there was water everywhere.'

'Julie?' Sienna nodded several times before adding in a low voice, 'Oh, yes, of course. That would be Maria's waitress.' Her twice broken heart twanged a little at the thought of Brett chatting up yet another young waitress when he had never wanted to talk to her, then twanged again. He was single. The waitress was probably single. None of her business. So why was it that she could not resist the temptation to tease *him* this time?

She lifted her head and made contact with those remarkable eyes, all thoughts of her wet feet forgotten. 'Well, *some* things seem to have changed! You actually *talk* to waitresses these days! I'm sure Julie was *very* informative!'

There was silence from the man standing only a few feet away from her across the wet cold tiles, and an electric spark of tension crackled through the air.

Then he dropped his head back, uncrossed his arms and let out a deep, rough belly laugh that echoed around the tiny space and vibrated through the floor and worktops. Her chair seemed to tremble with the force of it, and her toes clenched inside her moist shoes so that she would not tumble forward from her stool. Her soul, her heart and her mind filled with the joy of that deep, masculine chuckle.

It was the first time that she had ever heard him laugh, and at that moment she was seriously delighted that she had a worktop to hang onto. She tried to move back, away from him, but in this tiny kitchen there was nowhere for her to go. Her back was already hard against the patio chair.

She revelled in the sensation, her heart soaring, and for a second she was so, so, tempted to join him. She certainly needed a laugh after a day like she had just had.

The day she was still having, Sienna corrected herself. It was not over yet.

Deep smile lines creased the corners of his mouth, bringing his sparking blue eyes into startling contrast. It was intoxicating.

If she had ever thought that Brett could not be more attractive, he was doing his best to prove her wrong—without even realising he was doing it!

He leant forward until he was well and truly inside her personal space, and as he did so his hands came together so he could salute her with a slow clap. Once, then twice, before he moved back and ran his fingers through his short hair.

Then he looked across at her and broke into a wide grin. 'Relax, Sienna. The only girl who has me over a barrel is your aunt. She has me wrapped around her little finger and there is not one thing that I can do about it. I'd promise that woman anything. And she knows it.'

'What do you mean? Did she call you from Spain?'

'Actually, her friend Henry called, but I did have a chance to speak to the lady herself for a few minutes. The lovely Maria is way too busy chatting up the Spanish medics to spend time with me.'

Sienna blinked in surprise before clutching at her knees. 'Medics? What do you mean?' The remains of the tea sloshed onto the floor as she slipped the beaker onto the bench. 'Is Maria ill? Injured? How bad is it?'

Brett reached out and grabbed hold of her flailing hands.

'It was appendicitis. She was whipped into hospital straight away, has had the operation, and is now recovering among her friends from the dance club. She sounds *fine!* If anything she seems more concerned about you staying here alone than the fact that she has just had major surgery.'

'I did leave her several messages, but then the battery on my cellphone went flat. How is she? I mean, how did it happen?' Sienna asked, trying to slow her breathing and bring her heart-rate back to something close to normal.

Brett released her hands and leaned back on the worktop.

'Apparently she was on her way back from a banana boat race when the pain started. She slumped over in a Spanish dancing class and the instructor carried her to the ambulance. It was "*very* exciting", according to her friend Henry.'

'Banana boats? Exciting? Right. But that still doesn't explain why *you* are mopping her kitchen floor.'

'Ah,' Brett replied, his smile fading. 'Did you see the window?'

Sienna nodded. 'And the sign. How long have you been here?'

'A couple of hours. Long enough to know that Maria is in serious financial trouble and needs Rossi's to stay up and running while she's away— which could be a couple more weeks. She admitted as much just before her phone was confiscated. That's why she made me promise to do something for her.'

'Really? What was that?'

'Well, apparently you have many skills, Miss Rossi, but cooking is not one of them. Until Maria gets back, you're looking at her new chef!'

CHAPTER FIVE

Step 5: Add a Couple of Big Decisions...

SIENNA STARED in open-mouthed horror and astonishment as Brett gave her a jaunty salute and a cheeky wink before recrossing his arms and stretching out his long, long legs, only too aware that this snippet of news was going to take a while to sink in.

He was watching her now. Smiling. Totally confident and comfortable in his superiority. Just because he had announced that they were going to be trapped in this tiny kitchen together.

Trapped with Brett Cameron. Just the two of them. Together. *Alone.*

Her feet took a tighter grip on the chair inside her shoes. Making them squeak slightly.

He heard it and the smile widened.

How more infuriating and arrogant could this man get?

He had known that she was on her way here the whole time!

Known it before she had even got here! He had been expecting her to turn up!

But he still threw that water out of the door without a care about whether she would be standing there or not!

Well, she could change that quite easily. She had no intention of going back to the Manor, so *he* would have to be the one who made the move to…to whatever seriously important opportunity he was working on next as a superstar chef.

The crushing reality of the difference between their options hit her hard. Then hit her again.

Brett was a star. *Destined for great things.* And she was… Well, she was still Sienna Rossi, and she would take control of her situation as best she could.

'Thank you for volunteering to cook,' she blustered, in as calm a voice as she could muster under such extreme provocation, 'but that will not be necessary. I know a few retired cooks who would be happy to step in and help out. I can easily make a call tomorrow morning and have someone here in a few hours. Don't worry, I'll find another chef to take over in the kitchen. I'm sure that Maria would understand how busy you must be.'

Brett merely smiled indulgently at her discomfort and pushed himself to his feet. For one exciting and terrifying moment she thought that he was going to move even closer, but instead he turned back to the worktop, where she could see an assortment of cooking utensils and knives were laid out on a surprisingly clean white tea towel next to cartons of dried goods.

He casually picked up a moist poly chopping board and began drying it carefully with a paper towel before replying, his hands working the towel back and forth as he spoke.

'Sorry, but you don't get rid of me that easily. I'm not going anywhere.'

Those magical hands stilled for a moment as Brett looked intently towards her.

'Maria asked me to help with the cooking and that's what I'm going to do. I made a promise and I have every intention of keeping it. Besides, you're starting to hurt my feelings. If I didn't know better, I would say that you didn't want me here for the next two weeks. I am genuinely pained!'

Sienna clenched her teeth together in frustration. *Why was he not taking her seriously*? What did she have to do to persuade him to pack his bags?

'I'm sure Maria would understand that you have

important projects to be working on. Believe me. I can handle this.'

He acknowledged her words with a simple nod.

'I have no doubt that you can handle anything you set your mind to. And you're right. I flew in from Adelaide four days ago, and for the last three months a whole team of craftsmen have been tearing down a shell of a building and creating my first signature restaurant. The building work is behind schedule, and we're opening in six weeks. But from what I've seen, Maria Rossi needs help and she needs it now. I can afford to give Maria a few days out of my life to get this trattoria back on its feet. I owe her that. And I promised her I would do it. End of story.'

He turned sideways to face her and waved a packet of fusilli in front of her. 'Have you eaten this evening? Because I find it hard to think when I'm starving. Do you mind if I make something simple?'

Sienna bit down a quick reply. Lunch was a distant memory and she *was* hungry. And cold. And tired. And drained. At that moment pasta sounded pretty good. But she could *not* let him know how desperately she would love some hot food.

'I don't expect you to cook for me. And are you always so stubborn?'

'Always. And it is my pleasure. Oh, and, Sienna?'

The different tone of his voice was so startling that she flicked her head up towards him.

Too fast. The slight dizziness was back.

He winced at her before gesturing behind him with his head. 'One suggestion—and it is only a suggestion—before you make any decisions about taking on this bistro on your own, you might want to take a look into the dining room while I rummage around for something edible. That way we'll both be facing the horror of the situation.'

Brett swung open the refrigerator door and pretended to be examining the jumbled contents of the small freezer compartment as Sienna gingerly stepped on tiptoe past him into the corridor.

He had to keep his distance.

Not because Sienna scared him—she never had.

Not even when she'd been the family princess in the royal Rossi family and he very much the visiting peasant. Or at least that was how he had seen it at the time—no matter how much the family had gone out of their way to make him feel welcome.

He had been a boy from the wrong side of the tracks and kind-hearted Maria had taken pity on him when the academic world had labelled him a failure and turned its back on him.

Maria would have been horrified to know that he'd felt that way at the time. She had made it clear that the only reason he was in her kitchen—this very kitchen he was standing in now—was because of his talent. A talent she had believed in from the very first meal he had made for her. He might not have been able to express how he was feeling in words or on paper—but he had through his passion for food.

No. When he was around Sienna Rossi, *awe-struck* was a better description.

Brett pressed his back against the refrigerator door and looked around the kitchen where he had spent the best six weeks of his life. This was where he had eaten his first real Mediterranean food. Pasta which did not come ready cooked out of a tin. Tomato sauce made from fresh tomatoes and not from red plastic ketchup bottles.

For a teenage boy it had seemed as if a secret door had been opened into another world of endless delights and exciting new opportunities.

In that world he had found the potential to make something of his life without all of the labels he had managed to pick up over the years. Labels like 'difficult', 'sullen' and 'poor communicator'. 'Failure' and 'no future' had sometimes been added for good measure.

Apparently he had talent. All he had to do was prove it to others and convince them that he had potential. Face talking to trained chefs and persuade them to share their skills with him. Chefs like Frank Rossi and his family, who came from generations of skilled chefs and family cooks.

Frank and his sister, Sienna Rossi, had grown up with wonderful food and high expectations in a very different family from the one he was used to.

He had been so jealous of them back then it had been like a physical pain.

Little wonder that he had kept focused on what he'd had the power to control.

And yet here he was, back at Rossi's.

He turned back to the mini-freezer and his fingers closed over a plastic container with two large, brightly coloured dots stuck on the lid.

The air was sucked out of his lungs.

The red dot meant that this was a tomato pasta sauce, and the green dot told him that it was made using vegetables with herbs and spices. A basic sauce that could be used in a variety of recipes or served on pasta. No meat. No extras.

Unless she had changed her ideas, this was the same colour-code system that Maria has used all of those years ago, to hide the fact that she could not write or read well, and she was still using it now!

Brett carefully closed the freezer door and closed his eyes.

What was he doing here?

Chris needed him! The new business needed him! He should be working on his dream restaurant instead of mopping floors and defrosting pasta sauce!

What was he trying to prove by coming back to this kitchen where it all began? Maria wasn't here in person. And everywhere he looked in this tiny space caught him unawares.

Walking through that door tonight had brought it all back to him.

The uncertainty. The feelings of inadequacy he'd thought he had buried deep inside the outer persona he displayed to the world. It was all still there. Far closer to the surface that he had ever imagined.

And Sienna Rossi was partly responsible for making his world spin out of control.

He'd kept his distance from her tonight because of something he had not expected. Something which had hit him hard and hit him fast the moment he had swung open that back door and looked into her wide brown eyes.

Instant attraction.

Attraction which set his pulse racing and his heart thumping.

He had only ever felt that pull once before—the first time he had seen the most beautiful girl in Paris and been too terrified and stunned to even speak to her.

As usual he had covered up his true feelings with a cheeky smile and lively chatter—the happy-go-lucky attitude which had become his mask over the years to hide the vulnerable heart that he hid deep inside. Sometimes the mask fitted so well that it took a minor earthquake to make it slip a little.

And Sienna Rossi was certainly a seismic event as far as he was concerned.

The stunning woman in the fitted black skirt suit, designer shoes and tantalising smooth cream silk blouse was as far away from the plump, shy, teenage Sienna as he could have imagined. With her stunning good looks and elegant formality this Sienna was every inch the kind of head waiter that fine-dining restaurants would appreciate.

And that was the problem. He had just spent the last three hours fielding phone calls from Chris during his meeting with the architects, then cleaning up the mess in what had used to be a fine working kitchen—while all the time his brain had been in overdrive, conjuring up a vision of what a twenty-eight-year-old version of Sienna Rossi was going to look like.

Maria had told him that she was working as a head waiter and sommelier, but nothing could have prepared him for the woman who had been standing outside that kitchen door. Which for someone who took pride in their visual skills, he found deeply unsettling.

The suit, the uniform, the shoes. That was all surface gloss—designed to create the professional image fine-dining customers demanded when they were paying for the best. And Sienna certainly did it well.

Her long, straight, dark brown hair had always been tied back from a side parting, but from what he had seen of it tonight, even wet and un-brushed, she probably spent more to create that perfectly smooth, shiny, shoulder-length ponytail than he'd used to spend on clothes in a year at catering school.

She was stunning! Little wonder that his confidence had faltered. Perhaps he did not know who this version of Sienna truly was underneath that surface layer?

Except... It was her eyes that gave the game away.

He would have recognised those amazing deep caramel eyes anywhere—he had spent more than enough time staring at them over the dinner table at Rossi family meals, and then in the kitchen, where he'd never seemed to be able to escape her, no matter how hard he'd tried.

She had the most wonderful, gentle, feminine eyes.

He had certainly known plenty of women over the past ten years he had spent travelling the world—all wonderful, kind, generous and loving girls he had enjoyed spending time with as he worked hard to develop his skills.

But not one of them came close to having eyes like Sienna Rossi.

Eyes he could fall into and drown.

Those same eyes had been wide-open in shocked surprise when he had opened the back door—and even wider when he had deposited her onto the patio chair.

Eyes filled with tears.

Tears which had torn into his heart like sharp Japanese sushi knives. Shredding his mask of cheerful bravado into ribbons of need and regret and loss.

Eyes which could throw him off track in an instant if he allowed them. Combined with tears and the fiery mature woman who now lived beneath the austere black suit.

Dynamite. Absolute explosive dynamite.

Those eyes and those tears had sucked him back to a place he had not expected. A place where his heart was still open and he did not have to protect it from the pain of loss and regret.

She unsettled him.

Perhaps it was time to find out what kind of woman Sienna had become?

Time to light the blue touch paper and watch the firework display.

CHAPTER SIX

Step 6: A Valentine Wish...

THERE HAD been something in Brett's voice which had told Sienna that all was not going to be well, but she wasn't prepared for what lay in front of her after she squelched down the hall carpet and flicked on the lights in the dining room of Trattoria Rossi.

Or tried to. Three out of the four lightbulbs in the room were broken, and the one remaining red wall light gave out a positively eerie and pathetic glow, casting the dark, depressing and gloomy room into shadows.

Cold, frigid, damp shadows.

Sienna shivered and huddled deeper into the warmth of Brett's jacket before running her fingers across the old radiator. Icy cold. Terrific!

The central heating had not been turned on, and the cold wet February evening had combined with the wide expanse of glass window to create a distinct chill in the air which no amount of hot soup was going to put right, should a paying customer wander in from the street by accident.

Even the stone walls of the wine cellar in Greystone Manor were warmer than this space.

The only bright thing in the whole room was a handwritten poster, shining white and red in the light beaming out from the kitchen like a beacon in the murk around her.

Rossi's Famous Valentine Day Special Menus.

Oh, Maria! Valentine's Day! Of course! That made it even worse. Rossi's had used to be *the* place to bring your date on Valentine's Day.

Generations of teenagers from the local high schools had brought their first dates to Rossi's over the years. Maria had used to be booked from Christmas! And now look at it!

Valentine's Day? More like Halloween.

If Sienna had needed any more information about how low the restaurant had sunk, this was it. Just when she'd thought this day could not get any worse, she had to see this sad room. It was enough to start her off crying again, but she was not going to let Brett see her so out of control.

She felt humiliated! It was going to be hard

enough to face him after that pathetic display without more tears to add to her embarrassment.

But this was heartbreaking!

Maria should try and sell the restaurant and retire while she was still active enough to enjoy herself.

A shiver of cold and dread ran down her neck from a draught.

She was just about to slink back to her relatively warm kitchen chair when the telephone rang at the tiny table which served as reception desk.

Without thinking or hesitating Sienna switched back into head-waiter mode and took the call.

'Good evening, Trattoria Rossi. Sienna speaking. How may I help you?'

Her hand picked up the pen and flicked open the simple supermarket diary that was Maria's reservations book. Her hand stilled as she said, in as calm a manner as she could, 'Valentine's Day? Umm, let me just check for you.'

She took a breath, then another. Not because she wanted to keep the elderly gentleman on the other end of the telephone waiting by pretending that they were fully booked, but because of what she was looking at.

It was so remarkable that she actually held the book up into the light from the kitchen to check. She could hardly believe her eyes. But there was no doubt. Maria had not only taken bookings for Valentine's Day. She had taken *lots* of bookings. Easily enough to occupy three quarters of the tables.

'Oh, yes, I am still here. What's that? You've been celebrating Valentine's Day here for the last forty years? Well, yes, that is quite remarkable. Oh? You came to Rossi's on your very first date? That *is* lovely.'

Decision time.

Tell this nice gentleman that they were closed and likely to stay that way. *Or…* A totally crazy, outrageous and off-the-wall thought flicked into her mind.

She *could* do something remarkable. *She could stay.*

She could do this.

She could turn this dining room around. This *restaurant* around.

She had the skill, she had some time, and it would give her the boost to her confidence that she so badly needed.

There was a sudden clatter from the kitchen, followed by a smothered groan.

Of course she was going to need more than a little help with the food, and that would mean working with Brett Cameron.

On the one hand, he was obviously a wonderful chef, who was devoted to Maria—the food would be terrific, she had no doubt about that. And on the other he had clearly decided that he was going to be just as stubborn as she was!

She sighed out loud, and her shoulders slumped as the truth hit home.

In theory Brett Cameron and Sienna Rossi *could* be the best team Maria could possibly have hoped for.

They were both professionals with unique skills and talents. Two of a kind.

She owed it to Maria to make an effort and work with Brett. He had his own commitments, but was prepared to sacrifice them for Maria's sake. Surely she could find it in her to meet him halfway?

A smirking smile creased her mouth and she lifted the telephone closer. *Umm.*

Perhaps if she could succeed in working through a refurbishment plan with Brett then maybe, *just maybe*, she could work with Angelo or any other chef.

She would show Brett Cameron that she could put up with any challenge he threw at her.

And help sort out her decision making in the process.

Her head lifted and her voice suddenly sounded full of confidence. As though she was back in control, with a clear plan of what she wanted to do instead of being on the run. 'In that case I could not possibly let you down. Table for two. February fourteenth. Thank you, Mr Scott. I'll see you in… ten days' time. Have a lovely evening.'

Sienna gently replaced the handset and calmly added the reservation to the long list for February fourteenth.

She very carefully lowered the diary back onto the table, closing her eyes and trying to steady her nerves before going back into *that* kitchen.

Then the doubts started to creep back in. Threatening her resolve.

Things were happening far too fast for her liking.

First, she was on the run from Greystone and the mess that was the new chef, who might not have changed much from the arrogant *old* chef he'd used to be.

Second, the boy who had been her first crush was boiling water and reheating pasta sauce so they could have dinner together. And he was still the best-looking man she had ever met—any-where.

She was stuck here in the wreck of what had

used to be a stunning family bistro only a few short years ago. But it was either that or return to Greystone, while Brett struggled to cook and run her aunt's pride and joy on his own.

Sienna inhaled sharply and curled her toes inside her still moist shoes and stockings.

No way. Not going to happen.

She was here now and she had to make the best of it.

She could work with Brett and run the bistro for a week or two. Of course she could.

Time to get the team in place.

'Brett?' she called out as she squelched her way back through into the kitchen. 'What had you planned to do on Valentine's Day?'

'Come next week I'll be working like crazy on my new kitchen. Why do you ask? Looking for a date? You would be welcome in our spot in Notting Hill, only we are not *quite* ready to take guests at the moment.'

Sienna pushed her lips together and blew out hard. Notting Hill? That was where Angelo's had been. Her dream restaurant, in one of the most exclusive parts of London!

Of course Brett had been in Paris when all of that

had happened. He couldn't know about that part of her life. Good. Best to leave it like that.

She hid her painful moment by turning it into a wide grin. 'Notting Hill? Congratulations. Maria never said a word, although I haven't spoken to her since Christmas. Work has been mad. Thanks for the invitation, but I plan to spend the day a little closer to Rossi's. In fact, I want to spend it right here. Serving paying customers.'

His half-second delay in responding gave Sienna just enough time to make her bold move.

'It's one of her biggest nights of the year. I'm sure that she wouldn't want to turn away the business. Not on Valentine's Day. I only worked here once on Valentine's Day, to help her out, but it was good fun then and we could make it fun again.'

Brett stopped stirring and slowly turned around to face her. He looked straight into her eyes before he spoke, startling her so much that she fell back to her old nervous habit of twiddling at the antique silver ring she wore on the fourth finger of her right hand.

'You want to open up that freezing cold dining room and serve food to paying customers? On Valentine's Day?' His voice was low. Challenging.

'Yes,' she replied with a smile, suddenly desperate to turn the conversation around. 'Do you remember what it used to be like here? On Valentine's Day?'

'Hard to forget.' Brett pressed both of his palms flat on the worktop and his upper lip curved slightly to one side in a lopsided smile. 'Every one of my classmates was in here with his girl-friend, dressed in smart new clothes their mums had picked out for them. Pretending to be all so-phisticated and mature while all of the time they were squirming and itching with their ties and starched collars.'

He returned his spoon to the saucepan and slowly stirred from side to side, releasing the most deli-cious herby fragrance into the room. 'I was too busy burning my arms on their lasagne dishes and pizzas to catch a lot of the conversation, but Maria was bril-liant at making everyone feel at home and taking some of the nervousness out of their big day.'

Sienna watched Brett move between sink, worktop and hob. Fast. Slick. Practised. This was his life.

Pest. But a clever pest she needed to have on her side if she was going to pull this off. She was in control now; she would talk to him as though he was a colleague. That was all. A handsome, talented colleague who had the ability to make her dizzy.

'Exactly. That was what made Rossi's so special. Teenagers could come here for their first date and not feel intimidated. It might have been pasta and pizza, but it was served to them on a table with a tablecloth and napkins, in a real restaurant. I got the feeling that it was almost a rite of passage around here. Like buying your first car. That first date in Rossi's was something you would never forget—even if it did happen forty years ago.'

'Why, Sienna Rossi! I always *knew* there was a romantic streak in you! Where did *you* go for your first Valentine's Day date?'

'Sorry, I don't believe in romance any more,' she replied with a shake of the head and a dismissive sniff. 'And I think you can guess where I went. My dad wanted to keep a close eye on who, where and what was going on. I had no choice in the matter. And stop trying to distract me when I'm explaining why I couldn't say no to Mr Scott. Or any of the other couples who have booked for the evening. It's their special day. The fact that it is also good business is a bonus.'

'A-ha. Thought so. And I don't believe a word of it. Born romantic. Always have been. There is no use you trying to deny it. I do have one question. What will your current date think about you working on Valentine's Day?'

'My date? Oh. I'm between boyfriends at the moment. I always work through Valentines anyway. How about you?' Sienna asked, trying to sound casual. 'Do I need to keep a table for you and your lady friend?'

He smiled to himself. 'Not this year, thanks. Save the tables for gentlemen who want to show their ladies that they are special. *That* is what it is all about.'

'I agree with you. In fact...' Sienna ran her tongue over her lips before going on in a mad rush, desperate to get the words out before she lost her nerve. 'I was hoping that I could persuade you to be the guest chef for the evening. For Aunt Maria's sake. You *did* promise Maria that you would cook for her!' Sienna exclaimed in a louder voice than she'd intended to use.

Brett turned around to look at her, and tilted his head to one side before breaking into a wide smile.

'I did wonder where you were going on your trip down memory lane.'

He nodded once before turning back to the hob. 'Yes, I did make Maria a promise. And I keep my promises. The clock has already started ticking on my new venue. A few weeks from now there will be customers coming through the door. Not to mention top restaurant critics from around the world. I would only have a couple of days spare at most. Plus I have no kitchen, no menu and a massive loan to pay off. And do you know what?'

She held her breath. Waiting for him to come up with some totally credible and amazing reason why he could not possibly cook pasta and pizza for spotty teenagers and retired couples in a tiny bistro when he had a gourmet restaurant of his own to get ready.

He was Brett Cameron. Award-winning international chef. Not some catering student. Of *course* he wouldn't want to do the cooking himself. He probably had a whole brigade of minions at his beck and call.

What had she been thinking? Dreaming, more like.

She braced herself for the bad news. Why not one more thing to add to her disastrous day?

'Maria's sauce has been in the freezer since Christmas. It might have been delicious when it was made, but I've done the best I can to save it. Ready for some hot food? Then I'll tell you exactly how I plan to turn this place around in time for Valentine's.'

CHAPTER SEVEN

Step 7: Two Sparkling Brown Eyes...

BRETT PULLED OUT the ancient patio chair and patted it with one hand.

'Your table is ready, Your Highness. Sorry about the lack of fancy place setting, but I did disinfect the workbench while I was thinking up my master plan. It might not be up to fine-dining standards but it is clean. Providing, of course, you can lower yourself to eat at Maria's kitchen table? Just this once?'

One long, elegant tanned finger tapped the side of his nose, then he carefully folded the white tea towel over the crook of his arm like a silver-service waiter. 'It could be our little secret.'

'Funny. That's very funny,' Sienna replied, and squeezed her eyes together as she slid onto the chair. But he had already turned away to prepare their dinner.

A delicious aroma filled the space, and Sienna

lifted her head in curiosity to see what he had managed to conjure up from the meagre contents of Maria's stores. And was stunned by a very nice view of Brett's broad shoulders and snug cargo pants.

He was cooking her hot food.

Maybe she could forgive him, *just a little*, for trying to drown her.

'Tell me more about this master plan for *you* to turn this place around!' she managed to squeak out into the uncomfortable silence, trying to keep her voice light and joking. 'Have I missed something in the time it took me to freeze my feet in the dining room?'

He clearly took no notice whatsoever of the implied sarcasm about his bid for power, and a low rough chuckle echoed back from the plain painted wall he was facing as he cooked.

'I would hardly call it a master plan, but the building work on my kitchen has cut back the little time I have to work on the recipes for my signature menu.'

He pointed his stirring spoon towards his own chest, narrowly missing adding a smear of tomato sauce to his shirt as he did so.

'I have ten key dishes which are going to define what I'm trying to achieve.'

He paused, then turned back to the bubbling saucepan as he added a colander of drained pasta and gently folded it into the sauce to give it the lightest of coatings.

'Most chefs have three of four. Not me. I want ten perfect recipes for that first night. No arguments. And right now I don't have a kitchen to work in.' He raised the spoon to his lips before hissing, 'And this *still* needs more basil.'

Sienna watched in silence as Brett grabbed a bunch of wilted-looking green leaves from the dehydrated plant barely surviving in a terracotta clay pot on the windowsill, before moving back to the workbench and tearing them into narrow strips with strong deft fingers. Intense focused concentration, energy, excitement. All in those few moments it took to shred some basil which was certainly past its best and stir it into the sauce.

In that instant Sienna recognised the same boy she had known at sixteen. Oh, he might look different on the outside, with all the self-confidence and self-belief that a career as a superstar chef in the top kitchens around the world could bring. But there was no mistaking that flash of passion even in this simple task. He had never lost it. If anything he seemed to have developed it even more!

Brett Cameron in action was mesmerising. And somehow, amazingly, touchingly, a little vulnerable.

She envied him that self confidence.

Confidence enough to be able to create something remarkable no matter where he was working, and with ingredients that might not be up to his usual standard.

Suddenly her brain started to defrost like her feet, and she was instantly aware that Brett was still talking. The diverting pest of a man could multitask. *Rats*!

A steaming bowl of soft multi-coloured pasta with the most amazing fragrance wafted past her nose and onto a huge white under-plate on the worktop.

Her tastebuds kicked in the microsecond they savoured the herby tomato tang with a twist of…something she could not quite place. She was used to the best from the best. How could she not recognise that subtle smell? It had to be a special herb or spice. But which one?

She slowly inhaled the aroma of the sauce and closed her eyes in delight. Any thought of holding back on her enthusiasm to make Brett suffer was instantly blown away.

Drat the man for knowing exactly how he could

cut through the meagre defences she had built up! Perhaps it was this familiar and homely kitchen? Perhaps that was it? This was home.

'Basil, oregano, fresh rosemary. Garlic and onion with the tomato, and root vegetables and celery. But there is something else. I'm thinking dried chilli and marjoram?'

Brett was watching her with his fork poised to dive in. Waiting for her to try it first.

'I would recommend tasting some,' he said, with a satisfied smile in his low voice, and she took a breath. 'Or are you worried that you might like it too much?'

She opened her eyes, coated a single piece of pasta with the sauce and covered her lips around it.

'Wow,' she breathed, and chewed and swallowed with her eyes closed as pleasure flooded her senses. 'This. Is. Fantastic. Seriously good.'

Brett bowed slightly from his bar stool and dived into his own dinner, chewing through several mouthfuls in silence before gesturing towards her with his fork.

'I'm pleased you like it. Maria made the basic plum tomato paste, but the flavour was too bland for my taste, even with her choice of herbs, after a spell in the freezer. Hence the extras. Chilli flakes with a sprinkle of lemon zest. And fennel. Finely ground fennel seeds. No cheese.'

'Fennel seeds. That's it. That's the subtle richness. And I do like it. I like it a lot. Vegetarian dishes are always popular at the Manor.' Sienna chewed blissfully, aware that Brett was watching her as she ate. 'You could serve this sauce in so many ways. Very clever. And you're right. You don't need parmesan with this dish.'

'Absolutely. Of course it would have been better made with fresh ingredients. Wait until you try my three-mushroom cream sauce on fresh linguini. I'm still working on the best combination of dried and fresh mushrooms, but I'll get there. Or should I say *we'll* get there.'

He lowered his fork into his pasta bowl and leant forward, resting his elbows on his knees so that he could look into her face, his blue, blue eyes working their laser act on hers.

'I am a chef in need of a kitchen. Maria has a kitchen in need of a chef. It seems to me to point one way.'

The air crackled between them, and Sienna licked the sauce from her upper lip as her eyes locked onto his for one long, hot intense moment during which his eyes never left her face.

The heat from that gaze burnt away any lingering doubt she might have had that Brett Cameron had lost his ability to pull her from the real world and into the dizzy magical land where there was even the faintest chance that he might see her as someone he could care about.

'Go on,' she eventually managed to whisper.

'What if I agree to hire the bistro for the next ten days to work on my new recipes? It would mean closing the place to her regular customers, but I'll pay Maria the going rate for a commercial kitchen. Real money. Cash, if you like. What's more, I'll throw in a few extras to sweeten the deal.'

Sienna swallowed down her pasta.

'What kind of extras?'

'I owe Maria. And I can't work in a messy kitchen. Give me ten days and I promise you right here and now that I'll turn this place around. It's a winner. The lovely Maria gets a refurbished restaurant, publicity, and all the new kitchen equipment she wants. And our lovely girl can rest in her hospital bed knowing that her place is in good hands. What do you say? Do you think you can put up with me until Valentine's Day?'

* * *

Several hours later, Sienna sat on the edge of Maria Rossi's bed in the same shell-pink, first-floor bedroom which had become her safe refuge four years earlier, and ran the tip of her finger across the silver picture frame she had found on Maria's dressing table.

Laughing back at her from below the glass was a happy couple captured in time on one of the best days of her life. Sienna Rossi and Angelo Peruzi on the day they had opened their own London restaurant.

Angelo was so handsome in his chef's whites, with his dark curly hair and deep brown eyes. And that smile. That killer smile. How could she *not* have fallen for him?

They'd been young and in love and starting out on the greatest adventure of their lives together. Their own restaurant. Working together to create something amazing.

She had been so happy that day. So much to look forward to.

The Rossis had always loved their family photographs.

Perhaps that was why she hadn't been able to bring herself to destroy all of the other photos like this one, or lock them away out of sight in the special suitcase, along with the wonderful wedding plan and the lovely gilt-edged wedding invitations and the bridesmaid tiaras her future mother-in-law had sent from Los Angeles?

That special place where she had locked away her sensitive and loving heart.

Sienna dropped the photograph onto the bed and closed her eyes as the old familiar pain made her flinch. It was like a paper cut. Sharp. Deep. Only it could not be blinked away.

So what if she had survived the last four years by building tall, thick walls of prickly professionalism to protect her heart from that kind of pain? She needed those solid stone walls to give her some time to rebuild her confidence, so that she was capable and able to do her job without another control-freak chef.

Like Brett Cameron, for example.

Talking through his plans for the refurbishment work, she had come so close to dropping her guard that it scared her.

She was in serious danger of repeating all the mistakes in her life.

How could she fight the attraction to Brett and hope to win? He had all of the weapons he needed. Good looks, charisma, and a level of self-confidence that bordered on arrogance.

She was like a moth drawn to the light and heat of a fire. Destined to be consumed by the flames and fall to the earth and drown.

Only this time she didn't know if she had the strength to find her way back up to the surface for air.

She had to fight this attraction before things spun out of hand.

It had been four years since she had allowed anyone to take control, and look where that had taken her!

Maria had an awful lot to answer for! Even if this project *was* the distraction she needed.

All she had to do was survive the next ten days.

Then she would go back to Greystone Manor and face her past and her future. Alone.

CHAPTER EIGHT

Step 8: And a Pair of Pink Pyjamas

'TIME TO rise and shine!'

'Hmm. Who? What?'

Sienna pushed her nose out from below Aunt Maria's duvet and blinked several times before she focused on the wide shoulders of the tall, fair-haired man who was throwing back her curtains to let in the faint morning sunlight.

It was still raining.

'Oh, you have got to be joking…' she muttered, before pulling the duvet back over her head with a yawn. 'Why are you in my room? Go away!'

'And a very good morning to you too, sleepy-head.'

A long tanned finger hooked over the duvet cover, so that her eyes were just exposed, and she squinted up at the handsome, square-jawed blond who was grinning down at her.

He was shaved, his hair was still moist from the shower, and he smelt like every man should smell first thing in the morning. Fresh, clean, newly laundered, and radiating enough levels of testosterone and pheromones to make any half-drowsy girl want to drag him down under the covers with her.

If they could bottle that smell it would only be available on a medical prescription.

She inhaled another whiff. Free sample.

'I popped in earlier to check what you wanted for breakfast but you were still dreaming of Greystone Towers, so this is your first and only treat of the day. A lie-in.'

He pulled the duvet a little closer to his chest and leant forward, so that he could pretend to peer down under the cover.

'Lovely outfit, by the way. I can see that your fashion sense is still as stylish as ever.'

She instinctively reclaimed the duvet with both hands and pulled it tighter around her chest, to cover up the thick pink-and-white cotton pyjamas that she had found in Maria's wardrobe.

'It was freezing last night. Morning. Whenever I finally managed to get to bed. You might have noticed that the central heating is turned off.'

'Now I *am* offended. I am just across the hall,

you know.' He gave her a saucy wink and a quick salute before sitting down uninvited at the bottom of her bed.

'Oh, please. Don't beg. It's embarrassing. And what are you doing, coming in here so early? Or is it very late?'

'Almost nine. I know.' He shook his head from side and side and tutted loudly in faked disgust. 'Hard to believe that anyone can sleep this late. You have special dispensation this morning, but don't think you can get away with this behaviour for the rest of the week. Lots to do, girl!'

'Get away with it? Hang on just a minute.' Sienna shuffled up higher against the headboard, but tugged the covers up over her chest, much to Brett's amusement. 'It was your idea to start working on the master plan straight after dinner! I left you at about one this morning with your head in the oven. Don't you ever sleep?'

'Not much.' He shrugged. 'A couple of hours are quite enough. Besides...' and he patted the bedcover twice for effect before grinning up at her '...I am totally jazzed by our little project. The phones have been buzzing since dawn. There are guys all over London loading vans with tools and catering equipment as we speak.'

'Guys? Equipment? I'm confused. I thought you had only just arrived back in London.'

He nodded in acknowledgement. 'See, I *knew* that you were secretly paying attention while you finished off that second bowl of pasta. My mate Chris is in charge of the building work at my new place. I think he calls himself the project manager, or some other fancy title, but Chris knows who to call when he needs tradesmen, and at this time of year there are usually a few guys who need the extra work or a small job. So I made a few calls. Just to get things moving. This place is going to be jumping with workmen in a few hours, and it might be better for them if you are wearing something less alluring.'

Her chest rose and fell as words failed to form inside her still sleepy head, and she faltered slightly before sitting back.

Sienna closed her eyes, took several deep breaths, and tried to steady her pulse which was racing as anger and frustration surged through her body.

She could feel stiffness building in her shoulders, and tried to clench her toes under the covers.

It has already started.

She should have known and trusted her instincts the night before.

He was already giving orders. Taking control and telling her how things were going to be.

How could she have been so stupid? Why hadn't she stuck to her guns and made him leave?

Stupid, stupid girl. Pulled in by a pair of wonderful blue eyes and Hunk of the Month sex appeal being wafted in front of her over a hot meal!

She should have known that Brett Cameron was too dangerous for her!

For a few hours she had allowed herself to let down her guard.

Well, that was last night. When she'd been cold and exhausted. Not now. Not today. Not any day. Maria was her aunt and she was going to sort out these problems on her own. She didn't need Brett Cameron telling her what to do and how to do it.

Sienna gulped down a huge lump of resentment and disappointment before daring to use her voice. Trying to keep calm. In control without being aggressive. That was the key.

Whatever signal she was giving out, Brett had dropped his grin and now sat in silence on her bed. Watching her with a smiling face designed to weaken her resolve.

'When we talked this through last night,' Sienna managed to say in a low, calm, matter-of-fact voice, 'I thought that we were going to work on this project *together*. Agree the plan of action *together*. You focus on the kitchen and I work the dining room—but we both make sure that the other person is involved in any final decisions. That was what we agreed.'

She paused and licked her dry lips before going on. 'Sorry, Brett, but this is not going to work out after all. There are other kitchens you can rent to test out your recipes, and I can hire another chef to finish the work here on my own. Thanks for your ideas, but I truly don't think we can work together.'

His face twisted into a frown for a few seconds before he replied in a low, intense voice. 'What's the problem? Don't you trust me to call a few contractors to come in and do the work? I might have been out of town for a few years but I trust Chris. His guys won't let us down.'

Sienna shuffled higher up the bed and leant forward, her eyes fixed on his. This infuriating man was still not getting the message! 'No. It's not that at all.'

Brett crossed his arms and tilted his head to one side. 'Then what *is* the problem? You were asleep, we have the clock working against us, and we need to get this ball rolling. Come on—spill. Because I am not leaving this room until I find out what the matter is. And you already know how stubborn I can be when I have a mind to do something. So start talking.'

The problem? The real problem was probably already on his way back from California to take over as head chef at Greystone Manor, but she could not even *think* of Angelo right now!

'It's not you, Brett. It's how you work. I had a problem with another chef a few years ago, who let me down very badly. Since then I don't like being left out when big decisions are being made.'

She paused and gauged his reaction before going on.

'I don't like being sidelined. And I really don't like someone *telling me* how things are going to happen on a project I feel responsible for without asking me first. That is not what we agreed to do. I really cannot work this way. I'm sorry, but it might be better if I hired another chef.'

The muscles in Brett's arms flexed several times, and the thumping in Sienna's chest increased as the silence stretched out between them.

Maria *had* asked Brett to help—she believed him on that point. But the Brett she had asked to help was not the same Brett who had been a willing trainee years ago.

Far from it.

He was an intense, powerful man who was sitting on her bed.

That in itself would unsettle any female with a pulse.

His deep blue eyes were looking at her with intelligence and insight…and something else she could not put her finger on. Disbelief?

Her stomach clenched. Maybe she had over-reacted, as he'd said. But it had taken her four years of hard work to build up her cool and controlled exterior. She couldn't allow Brett to knock away her carefully constructed barriers in only a few hours.

He was probably thinking that she was a spoilt brat who was too used to having her own way. And she had just presented him with a get-out clause—on a silver platter.

Brett Cameron perched on the end of Sienna's bed and watched her clutch the bedclothes tighter up around her chest.

She was trying to get rid of him.

Why? All he had done was get the work started while she slept!

What was she so afraid of? Losing her independence?

Or something more fundamental than that?

Why was she so worried that he had leapt ahead? What had this other chef done that was so terrible that she couldn't trust *him?*

He caught her eyes at that moment, and the reality of her fear shone through in a brief moment before she looked away, but too late. She had told him what he needed to know. She had been seriously let down by someone she had trusted—that much was obvious.

This was not the bossy self-centred, always right and very demanding princess talking; this was a frightened woman at the end of her tether.

Well, he could do something about that! If Sienna needed reassurance, that was what he would give her.

'You don't need to hire another chef.' He raised one hand and let it fall to the bedcover.

His next words took her breath away.

'We've all been let down by people at one time or another. You want to be part of the decision process. I can understand that. But I told you yesterday I am not going anywhere! So you're stuck with me…although I *have* been keeping things from you which you are going to find out one way or another.'

The side of his mouth crinkled up to match the creases beside his entrancing eyes, and the tension she had not even realised was between them cracked like a flash of lightning.

She could not help herself. The heated exchange was gone with his smile, and she brought her brows together in mock concern. 'It must be very serious.'

He snatched a breath and shook his head from side to side. 'Oh, it is. Sad case. Thing is…well, I know I can be very impulsive. I desperately need someone around who can point my idiot enthusiasm in the right direction. Think you can cope with that, Miss Rossi? Give me another chance to prove that we can work together?'

His eyes gave the game away, of course. Nobody with those blue, blue twinkling eyes could possibly be taking himself seriously. But Sienna raised her eyebrows slightly when he added, 'Or am I way too much for you to handle?'

'Oh, I think I can handle you quite well, Mr Cameron. Quite well indeed.'

'Good to hear it. Because—again—I am not going anywhere. I made Maria a promise and I keep my promises. Especially to pretty ladies.'

He stretched out his long, denim-clad legs and eased off the bed in a smooth rustle of muscle and suppressed energy.

'I'm going to take my second breakfast in the bistro, so we can start work straight away.' And then he half turned back to smile at her with a cheeky grin. 'If that it is okay with you…boss?'

He dodged out of the way as Sienna's pillow came flying towards him.

CHAPTER NINE

Step 9: Sprinkle with Pink Flamingos

'YOU HAVE A checklist. I like it.'

He also liked her perfume, her flash of a smile and the way their bodies brushed up against one another as they manoeuvred their way around Maria's kitchen like ballet dancers, in some complex, unrehearsed choreography which only the two of them could come up with.

He really, really liked the way she looked in the morning, with her hair loose and messed up on the pillow, one arm flung out on top of the bedcover. Men had striven for years to paint women who looked so naturally beautiful. He had enjoyed a moment of guilty pleasure alone before she'd stirred and he tiptoed out of her room in stockinged feet to wake Chris up with an early morning telephone call, desperate not to disturb her.

Whatever demons had driven Sienna Rossi out onto the streets of London late on a wet, cold February evening would not go away after a few hours' sleep, but he wasn't the one who would drag them from her. If Sienna wanted to tell him why she had sought refuge at Rossi's out of the blue like that, that was fine, but he would not press her.

All he knew was that Sienna needed to be here, working, keeping herself busy to escape the inescapable—and he knew about that method. Only too well.

Besides, staying longer in that bedroom would have been seriously bad for his ability to keep his hands off her.

She'd been stunning then and was still stunning now, dressed in simple beige trousers and a light sweater the colour of ripe purple plums, with that lovely chestnut hair smoothed and sleek, pulled back behind her head and gathered inside a wide silver clip.

She looked up at him, her pen poised over the pink pad of writing paper she had found in the drawer in Maria's dressing table. Her pink pen had a jaunty pink flamingo made of bouncy rubber stuck on the end. He would have pulled it off the moment he laid eyes on it, but somehow the paper and pen were so perfectly matched it seemed a shame to spoil the set.

Oh, yes, he also liked the way she savoured and enjoyed every mouthful of food that passed her lips. Those slim hips must come from the most excellent of genes and a frantically busy life.

Time to think about something else, before he started cooking just to tantalise her with exciting new flavours and foods.

One thing was for sure. He was already looking forward to seeing this woman eat something extra special that he had made just for her. And soon.

'A girl needs a list,' she replied, before biting into a thick, crunchy piece of buttered toast made from a fresh loaf of unsliced granary bread he had bought from the local bakery at some silly hour of the morning. 'Where's *your* list? I need to know what you've been up to when I wasn't around to supervise.'

He tapped the side of his temple several times with his third finger.

'All in here. Shall I start while you eat? Great. Here are my top three priorities.'

He raised his left hand and started with his thumb.

'The cracked window needs to be replaced. My

pal Chris is on the case. The glaziers we are using for my building work will be around this afternoon to take the measurements and—you are going to like this—they can etch the glass with anything you like and have it fitted within forty-eight hours.'

His right hand swished through the air. '"Trattoria Rossi."' Then he followed through with a sigh and a grin. 'Problem is that I mentally tuned out the minute the glazier started talking about fonts and layout. We need something classy, but simple. But also fun and easy to read. Big letters.' He gave her a half smile before confessing, 'That's the dyslexia for you. I have no clue.'

There was a sudden intake of breath and a stunned silence from across the kitchen.

'Dyslexia? Are you serious?' Her voice was so full of genuine surprise and concern that he turned to face her.

'Didn't Maria tell you?'

'Not a word. I am so sorry, Brett, I had no idea!'

He shrugged and slipped his toasted cinnamon-and-raisin English muffin onto a plate, before sliding onto the stool on the other side of the table from Sienna, who had stopped eating and was watching him with wide-eyed interest and concern, her toast halfway to her mouth.

He tried to dissipate the tension by taking a bite out of his breakfast and waving the muffin around before answering.

This wasn't the time to tell her the truth about how hard it was living day to day with dyslexia. And he certainly did not want her pity.

So down came the mask as he made light of the whole sorry mess that was pain and frustration, living in a world of words and letters which made little sense to him. Normally he had admin staff and Chris to take care of the paperwork side of the business. Not here. Not at Rossi's.

Here he was, back to being on his own. Without even Maria to help him work through a raft of coping mechanisms.

Unless Sienna helped him over the next few days he would be floundering, just as he had been the first time he came to work here.

And that made him feel even more inadequate than ever.

'It's no secret that I have dyslexia,' he replied in a casual voice. 'The Australian press caught hold of it a while back, and I was invited onto several TV shows. You know the sort of thing.' His hand came up and scribbled a title in the air. '"How I overcame my terrible disability and how it made me a better person."'

He sniffed dismissively and took a sip of coffee. 'I was amazed by how many people have some form of dyslexia and wanted me to talk to them about it. Luckily I had an excellent excuse. Work! So now you know. Making lists and sign painting are not among my special skills and will need to be assigned elsewhere.'

He lifted his head and pretended to look at her list, keen to change the topic. *Now*! His plan worked, as she flapped the paper at him before replying.

'Ah. Now you're trying to be modest. And failing miserably. I am even more staggered by how much you have achieved since the last time we met,' she teased in an amazed voice, before scribbling something on her pink paper, the rubber flamingo jiggling madly as she did so. 'Window-etching in the dining room. Got it. And thank you for your honesty. Now I know, it helps me to see which jobs I have to do.'

He grinned back in reply and seized upon the opportunity to change the subject. 'Teamwork. Right? You handle the window-etching, and in exchange I volunteer to help take out the old dishwasher and fit a replacement. The good news is that the dishwasher from the restaurant we are ripping apart is still on site, and it looks positively new compared to this baby. It should fit, so Maria gets it for free.'

Sienna smiled and waved her toast in his direction. 'Heavy equipment? All yours. Even better when it's a freebie. What's number three?'

He was so dazzled by her unexpected smile that it took a moment for him to reconnect.

'The other good news is that both the oven and hobs work, in their own fashion—they've been replaced some time in the past five years—and the fridge is fine. Except…'

Her last morsel of toast was being crunched noisily. 'Except?'

'Most of the ingredients in the fridge and storeroom are either out of date or I wouldn't want to use them. So I need to go food shopping today. More coffee?'

Sienna shook her head. 'I've already had more than I normally drink in a day. The caffeine rush is starting to kick in. Although I needed something to lift my mood after seeing the dining room in daylight.'

She winced and hunched her shoulders before giving an exaggerated shudder.

'Okay, those were my suggestions. Hit me with *your* top three,' he replied, before draining his own espresso.

Sienna tapped on her clipboard, and the flamingo looked as if it was trying to take off.

'Bad news first. The dining-room walls need to be repaired and repainted. They are *so* tired and in need of loving care and attention—but there are special chemicals to help lift the stains. That is my first job.'

She flicked up a glance towards Brett. 'I am going to need help emptying the room. This actually might be a bigger job than I expected. The carpet squidges and squelches when I walk on it. I don't want to even *think* of what has been spilt down there over the years. No more carpet. I would suggest hard flooring, but I'll get back to you with some options as soon as the carpet is gone.'

Her hand paused before the flamingo had time to rest, and her bright, open-eyed face looked up at him.

His heart thumped at how her face and personality beamed back at him for that microsecond, before the serious professional Sienna he had met the previous evening got back to the task.

'Most of the chairs can go out with the carpet! There are only about four I would trust with my weight. The rest are only fit for firewood. Discount warehouses should have what we need.

And forget the tablecloths and napkins. Burnt, stained or torn. Darning is not one of Maria's finer skills.' Sienna shuddered before going on. 'I've already thrown them out.'

Brett groaned. 'So basically we don't even have a dining room. Wonderful. Is there any good news? At all?'

She thought for a second before nodding. Once. 'The tables are basically sound. I think Maria inherited them when my parents sold their restaurant a few years ago. I can use them. And I called Frankie at the deli—he says hi, by the way—and apparently there are boxes of old stuff from the restaurant which Dad kept as spares still stashed in my parents' basement. They have been there for ages and he is happy for us to salvage what we can since it is for Aunt Maria. I think that could be a good place to start.'

'Aha. You see? You *do* need me after all.'

She sighed dramatically before replying, instantly taking the wind out of his sails.

'Sorry, but Frankie is busy in the deli and the boxes will need to be lugged up narrow stairs. I need someone who is not frightened by either mutant spiders or heavy boxes, and you're the closest I have to a lugger type. So I'll have to make do.'

'Faint praise, which I accept none the less. So. When do you want to go back to your parents' house?'

CHAPTER TEN

Step 10: Add Hot Pink Psychedelic Flowers

'WELL, THIS is going to be weird. I haven't been back to the Rossi family house in years. Pity your folks are on holiday. I would have liked to say hello!'

'Caribbean cruise. A late Christmas present from the family. According to Frankie they are putting up with fancy cocktails and evening dress in glorious sunshine. Mum is having a wonderful time.'

Brett stared out at the lashing rain between the swish of the car windscreen wipers, and sighed as he turned into the small drive outside the Rossi house. He sat back, drumming his fingers on the steering wheel to the beat of the music playing on the car stereo and the rhythm of the wipers.

'Glorious sunshine! Don't remind me. Adelaide is lovely in February. But, hey, I'm going to be around for the long term. I'll make sure that their names are on the guest list.'

He glanced sideways just as she half turned to him with a distant smile and distractedly replied, 'Mmm. They would love that. Especially if some of the dishes are based on Italian classics. My dad would enjoy telling you how to cook them properly.'

Then she realised what she had just said, and fidgeted even more in the slippery leather passenger seat so that she could sit a little taller.

'Sorry. That came out in completely the wrong way. If the rest of your Italian dishes are anything like that amazing pasta sauce you concocted last night, they will be totally thrilled. Did you know that your name actually came up during Christmas lunch? One of my cousins was in Adelaide and ate in your restaurant. He went so far as to say that the food was excellent. Maria was very proud.'

Brett felt a blush of heat at the base of his neck and shuffled awkwardly. 'She never told me that.'

Sienna faced forward, staring at the house, oblivious to his discomfort as she twiddled her silver ring. 'Well, it would be awful if you developed a swollen head.'

He acknowledged the possibility with a low chuckle, and undid his seat belt so he could focus on the lady by his side, who had remained silent for most of the journey from Maria's.

Between Trattoria Rossi and her old home her get up and go had got up and gone. No sparkle. No fizz. Nothing.

Sienna stayed where she was.

Then, conscious that he was looking at her, she lifted her head and straightened her back, as though she was preparing to go for a job interview instead of visiting the house she had grown up in and called home for most of her life. She glanced up at the front door through the rain and bit her bottom lip. Her bravado faded with her smile.

Some part of Brett reminded him that Sienna's private demons were none of his business. But the girl who had burst into tears when he had soaked her lovely shoes last night was right back in the car with him now. Frozen in her seat.

She was scared! Well, he knew just what that felt like. She needed help and he was right there. As he had told her, he wasn't going anywhere.

'I hate to criticise any lady's footwear, but those are so *not* you.'

Sienna blinked several times at him, and then stared hard at her feet. Maria Rossi's short Wellington boots stared back at her. They were purple, with psychedelic white and hot pink flowers. The only vaguely waterproof item of footwear in Maria's extensive shoe collection. She might fit the same size of shoes as her aunt, but style was another matter completely.

'I would have gone for the yellow daisy sandals I found on top of the refrigerator and put up with wet feet—but, hey, that's who I am,' Brett added, in as casual a voice as he could muster, and shrugged.

She looked up from her boots and stared into his face. Those deep brown eyes that he had admired for so long locked onto his and would not let him go.

Sienna Rossi was holding onto his strength and positive energy every bit as much as if he had been physically holding her in his arms.

And the unsettling feeling swelled into something much bigger.

The only sound in the car was the swish swish of the wipers and the low beat of a Latin dance band for a few long seconds before she gave a weak, fragile smile.

'I did leave some shoes in my old bedroom. And a change of clothes. I should go and get them.'

'Absolutely. Stay right there for a moment, and we'll get ready to make a run for it!'

Sienna watched Brett shrug into his jacket, grab a golf umbrella from the backseat and fling open the car door before dashing out into the lashing rain with a shout. She barely had time to release her seat belt and grab her bag before Brett was opening the door and reaching inside for her to join him.

She let out a long, calming breath and swung her legs out of the car—into the largest puddle she had ever seen in her life. Brett was already beside her, his hand on the small of her back, drawing her closer to his warm body under the shelter of the huge umbrella.

Without thinking or hesitating, she wrapped her right arm around the waist of his jacket and huddled closer, so they could run for the shelter of the wide porch which covered the entrance to the front door.

Yelping and laughing like children, they dodged the puddles and the wet bushes which blew against their legs in the brisk wind. At last they reached the shelter of the stone arch and Sienna immediately started shaking the rain from her hair, grateful to be out of the downpour but reluctant to leave the safe embrace of the man whose hand was still on her back as he closed the brolly one-handed.

His life and passion and energy were exactly what she needed.

Coming back home shouldn't be a big deal, but

it was. A *very* big deal. And she was grateful that he was there with her.

'Made it,' Brett joked. 'Maybe those boots were a success after all!'

His warm body was still pressed against her side, and he did not appear to be in any hurry to separate, so she had to twist inside his arms to look at his face, her raincoat sliding smoothly against his padded jacket. His hand drew her closer, so that when the palms of her hands came up to press against the front of his jacket there was nowhere else to look but into his face.

Close up and in daylight it was like seeing a stunning landscape at close range.

The tiny thin white scar that cut his heavy blond left eyebrow.

The slight twist on the bridge of his nose which told her that it had been broken at least once.

And his eyes. The blue was not one solid colour but a mosaic of different shades and variations, from almost white through cobalt, to dark navy and everything in between, each tiny dot subtly different from the others. And they were all looking at her with an intensity and strength and yet a vulnerability that told her far more about the real Brett Cameron than he probably would have liked.

Playing with fire could get you burnt. *And that look was incendiary.*

Her hands pressed a little harder before lifting away. Half of her already missed the warmth and intimacy of being so close to a man like Brett, while the other part shook its head in disgust and reminded her that she had been down this road before with a chef. And look where *that* had got her!

Chef magnet. She hated it when Carla was right.

How many times had the sixteen-year-old version of herself dreamt of being held by Brett Cameron? And here she was, snuggled up with only a few layers of clothing between them. Back home. Back where she'd started. Apparently none the wiser for twelve more years of life.

Time warp.

She was in danger of losing control just when she needed all of the discipline she could muster.

Brett could never know how this house she had once loved with such a passion had become a virtual prison. Her old childhood bedroom a place of nightmares, where she'd spent so many dark and depressed days wallowing in defeat and despondency after Angelo had abandoned her, taking her hopes and dreams and confidence with him.

If Maria had not offered her an escape route, she would probably still be living here!

'Basement. Do you remember where it is?' she finally managed to ask, in a voice which sounded horribly squeaky against the rattle of the sleety rain.

Brett practically snorted in curt reply. 'Shall we try downstairs?' he said, but slid in beside her as she turned her key in the lock. 'Your dad had me running up and down those stairs for days when I first started. I remember every moment I spent in this house. They were some of the best weeks in my life. Allow me to lead the way.'

CHAPTER ELEVEN

Step 11: And a Box of Warm Memories

'AND WHO is this again?' Brett asked, holding up a very battered black-and-white print of a handsome dark-haired young man in a starched white apron with his arms folded across his chest. 'I'm starting to lose track.'

'Great-Uncle Louis. He was one of the original Rossis who came over from Tuscany to open the very first ice cream parlour in this part of London.'

'Fine moustache. What was the ice cream like?'

'He was horribly proud of that moustache and used to wax it every day.' She shuffled with her bottom along the step, and looked around conspiratorially before leaning in to whisper in Brett's ear. 'The hair wax tasted better than the ice cream. In fact, I think it was the same recipe. But you can't tell a soul.'

'My lips are sealed.' He smiled. His left side was squeezed tight against her from hip to shoulder, but he made no attempt to move to a more comfortable position on the narrow wooden stairs leading down to the Rossis' basement. 'Good old Great-Uncle Louis is still going to look wonderful in the Rossi gallery. Maria is going to love it. Great idea.'

Sienna bit her lip to hide her pleasure, and tried to deflect the attention away from herself. 'The Rossi restaurants have always had family photographs on the walls. I know it seems a bit kitsch now, but as far as Dad was concerned the restaurant was an extension of his own private dining room, and that meant you had your family around you. You know that Frankie has even more boxes of photographs at his place?'

Brett looked around the jumble of boxes and crates in amazement. 'There are more?'

She laughed and waved the folder of photographs they had selected together. 'I think twenty is enough for what we want. Modern picture frames and plain cream walls are going to make these pop. Wait and see.' She smiled up at Brett, only his attention had been taken with a large colour print which he seemed to be examining in great detail. 'Who's that photo of?' And then she caught a glimpse. 'Oh, no. I thought I had destroyed all the remaining copies. Pass it over!'

She made to grab at the offending item, only he swiftly passed the photograph to his other hand and held it at arm's length, high in the air.

'My, my, Miss Rossi. You *do* make a pretty bridesmaid. Is this Frank's wedding?'

She groaned and sat back, with her head in her hands.

'I was shanghaied, kidnapped and sold down the river. Pale green is not my colour. I don't think it is *anyone's* colour, but my future sister-in-law loved it. No choice in the matter.'

'Oh, I don't know…the ruffles are *very* fetching. Perhaps you should wear them more often?' he replied, with a waggle of his eyebrows.

'Oh, please. Like *you* are a fashion guru. I'd like to see your old family photos one of these days. Or do you keep them under lock and key in some bank vault where they can't be used for blackmail?'

His laughter came straight from the gut, and echoed around the long, narrow basement and through the stairs until she could feel the vibration of sound through every bone in her body.

'Sorry to disappoint you, but if there ever were any photos, they are long gone. My mother and I were never much for family gatherings. She was too busy moving from one rented place to another to keep in touch with any relatives we might have had in Scotland, and I certainly can't remember any photos on the walls.'

He glanced sideways at her over his shoulder, with that lop-sided smile he did so well. 'When you are living out of a suitcase, you soon learn to carry only what you need.'

The fluorescent strip lighting overhead in the basement created harsh shadows and dark corners where Sienna knew monster mutant spiders liked to lurk. But looking into Brett's eyes she saw only the type of honesty and frankness that made the breath catch in her throat.

He was telling her the truth and he did not expect her to feel sorry for him. Just the opposite! The way he spoke was so matter-of-fact it was as though he told perfect strangers about his difficult past every day of the week!

It must be wonderful to be so confident and open to the world.

How did Brett do it?

How did he open his life up to such scrutiny?

And how, of all of the people on this planet, was he the only person *she* wanted to open up to? She *wanted* to tell him the truth about Angelo. Not the half-truths that her friends and family had passed around to cover up the whole sordid mess!

Even scarier, she *needed* him to know the truth. The poisonous secrets she kept within her hung like a thick security screen between them, just as they had with every other man she had come close to in the past four years. Except Brett was in another league. The boy who had been her first crush had dropped into her life less than a day earlier, and she already felt as though she had known him as a friend for years. The friend she'd never had.

Maybe that was it? Maybe she wanted to have a second chance to be friends with Brett? She had been too scared and intimidated the first time around to make the move to start a conversation, and he had been so withdrawn and obsessive back then.

Was it possible that she could take a risk and form a real friendship in the few days they would be working together at Maria's? It was probably the only chance she would ever have. One way or another they would soon be heading back to their real lives and jobs, where they would be destined to meet up on rare social events, if at all, when they would be surrounded by other people.

'I don't like it when you go quiet on me. Tell me what you are thinking,' Brett asked.

Not on your life.

'I was just wondering what it felt like to be dropped into the madness of the Rossi household when you took the job here. It must have caused you permanent psychological damage! We do tend to be a little exuberant when a few of us get together!'

He looked at her. Really looked at her. With an intense focus that made her fight the temptation to squirm away on the hard step and sit on her hands.

'I've carried your family with me every second since the day I left this house and the Rossi restaurant. They taught me everything I needed to know about what a family should be like, and I'll never forget it. They were great! Best six weeks of my life. I lived for that kitchen and those family meals on Sunday afternoons.'

Sienna stared at Brett open mouthed, and collapsed back against the step.

'You *lived* for them? The family meals that turned into yelling matches—or even fights when all my uncles were in town? You actually *liked* all of that? Most of my pals from school ran away, screaming!'

She squeezed her eyes tight shut and took

herself back to those huge family Sunday get-to-gethers, when all the relatives and distant cousins, plus visitors, plus catering crew, would be assembled around one huge extended dining table for several hours.

'The noise! How could you forget the uproar and the arguments? You *cannot* have loved the noise of ten kids and a dozen adults all competing in decibels and speed to get attention! We were all exhausted, deafened and hoarse by Sunday evening. It was manic.'

'You've forgotten to mention the food.'

'Okay, the food was fantastic—but it was still manic!'

'The food wasn't just fantastic. The food was *amazing*. The best. I worked in those kitchens all week, but nothing came close to the wonderful meals your dad made for his family on Sundays. I never expected to be invited to join in, but, *wow,* I was so grateful for the experience. It took me weeks to work out what made it taste so delicious.'

'He always invited the kitchen crew to be part of our Sunday meals. But what do you mean about the food tasting different? Did he try out different recipes on us?'

'No, nothing like that.' He sat back against the

wall and hitched one of his legs up, so that he was facing Sienna with his leg down one side of the step and his arm wrapped around his knee.

'It was the love. Every single dish your dad served was made with such love for the people around his table you could almost taste the pleasure he'd had making wonderful meals for his family to enjoy. Didn't you sense that?'

'I suppose it was what I was used to,' Sienna answered, shocked by the emotional depth of what Brett was saying to her. She could hear the passion and fire in his voice, as though he was reconnecting to those Sunday afternoons.

'Exactly. You have to remember that until I started working for Maria my only experience of eating hot meals someone else had cooked were takeaway pizzas and school dinners. And—' he gestured to his chest with one hand '—I am an only child. Put those things together and being dropped into the Rossi family table was like jumping onto a moving roller coaster at a fun fair.'

She tried to imagine how her family must have appeared to someone who had not grown up with them and failed. Miserably.

'It must have been totally bewildering.'

'It was.' He chuckled. 'For the first two minutes

sitting at the table. Then Maria pushed a huge plate of antipasti in front of me, and slapped me on the shoulder, Frankie started talking about football, which caused an argument with one of your cousins who supported another team, and suddenly the foccacia was flying everywhere and your parents were laughing their heads off.'

Brett paused and picked up the photo of Frank's wedding, so that Sienna's attention was diverted away from his face when he spoke again in a soft voice tinged with feeling.

'I felt like I had come home. Even though I had never experienced a big family home it was what I had always imagined it would be like. I was completely and absolutely at home.'

Sienna sat in stunned silence. Brett had found his home within her family. While she hadn't been able to wait to leave it when the going got tough.

How had that happened?

Brett tapped the photo twice with his fingernail. 'Frank invited me to his wedding, you know. But I had just started a new job in Paris and couldn't get away. Shame that I missed it. I would have liked to see you in that dress.'

'Me? Do you even remember me from back then?'

'Of course. I remember you very well indeed.'

'I don't understand. You never said a word to me. Not one word. In the whole six weeks you worked as a catering student. I thought you didn't like me. Couldn't bear to have me around. I was far too shy to talk to you when I worked for Maria, but you could barely manage to say hello and even that was forced out of you. I was so crushed.'

His chest rose and fell, his lips parted, and without warning Brett stretched out his hand and took Sienna's fingers in his, lifted them towards him.

She tried to snatch her hand back. 'Hey! My hands are filthy from working in those boxes.'

'So are mine,' he replied lightly, not giving way. Stubborn.

She stared in silence as he gently turned her hand over, stretching out her fingers in the wide palm of his left hand, stroking the life line with the fingertip of his right.

The feel of that fingertip was instant, and so electric that she gasped out loud. It was probably the silliest thing she could have done.

Hot sensation hit her deep inside. Warmth and welcoming sensations she'd thought she had left behind for good on the day she'd stood at the departure gate and watched Angelo board his flight for California, knowing in her heart of hearts that she had lost him. The kind of heat that was addictive in small doses and killed you in larger ones.

No man had ever done this to her before with one touch of his hand, and she tugged to release herself before he could throw her life and her careful plans even more off balance.

'You see this beautiful hand? It's soft and warm. There are no cuts or burn marks or rough skin from scraping tons of vegetables and fish scales in freezing water.'

His fingertip moved further up her longest finger, stroking the whirls in gentle circles and prolonging the delicious torture she was totally helpless to resist or fight.

'I can see your fingerprint. The skin is so smooth it could be a child's. It is so lovely no man could possibly resist it. Including me.'

He lifted her hand closer to his face, and she sucked in a breath and closed her eyes as he kissed her palm.

'This is the hand…' his mouth moved over the bump at the base of her wrist with gentle pressure '…of a princess.' Then those lips pressed gently onto her pulse-point, the lightest of pressure. It made her quiver under his mouth, but if he felt it, he did nothing. He was far too busy kissing her wrist.

'I think Maria knew that I felt like an outsider from the wrong side of the tracks, but I was made welcome all the same. I envied you so much. You were born into a wonderful family and you seemed to take it all for granted. Have you any idea how angry that made me feel? How frustrated?'

His eyes locked onto hers.

'That's why I didn't speak to you, Sienna. I was jealous, angry and bitter. And I never once felt good enough.'

Heart racing, she swallowed down the apprehension and found her throat had somehow become completely dry.

So when her cellphone started to ring in her handbag it took only a few milliseconds for her to make the decision not to answer it. Especially when her bag was on the floor of the basement and it would mean breaking her contact with Brett to jog down the few steps and pick it up.

For the first time in a very long time she decided that some things were more important than answering her phone.

Brett shot her a grin, folded her fingers one by one over the spot where he had kissed the palm, and carefully lowered her hand to the floor—as though it was the most fragile, precious object in the world and any breakage would be on his bill.

The wooden planks felt cold and rough compared to the warmth of his fingers, and she shuddered with regret.

'The window guys will be wondering where we've got to.' He smiled at her with eyes that spread the warmth of those fingers all over her body. 'Ready to go?'

Nowhere near. There was music. She was hearing music when she looked at him.

No, she wasn't. It was the ringtone of *his* cellphone.

An operatic tenor was singing in Italian.

'That's probably them now. Excuse me.'

Both legs swung out, and in an instant he had flicked open the cover.

'Hi, Chris. Yeah. Great to speak to you, mate. Yes, we…er…found what we were looking for. It's a *real* treasure trove down here.'

He raised his eyebrows towards Sienna at that moment, and she instantly felt the heat from her blush send fire up the back of her neck.

'Tablecloths, napkins and loads of old family photos. The works. Sienna is really pleased. How are you getting on with that window?'

The smile on Brett's face faltered. 'Tell me you are kidding.'

The tense wire that had bound them together in the silence and intensity of the moment twanged. And snapped.

There was just enough of a pause for Sienna to blink hard, sit up and clasp hold of Brett's arm.

'You're not kidding. Sorry to hear that. Well, here's an idea. We can't let a measly thing like a flood prevent a little girl from having her birthday party, can we? Why don't you have it at Rossi's? I'll trade you one birthday party complete with balloons and entertainment, for one replacement window. Providing you can get the work done in time, of course, otherwise it might be a bit draughty. What do you say?'

The implications of what he was saying slapped Sienna in the last sensible part of her brain, and her fingers bit into his arm as she mouthed the word 'No' and sliced her right hand through the air in a vigorous cutting motion.

He ignored both. 'It's a deal. Thursday. Four o'clock. Looking forward to it. See you in three days. No problem, mate. No problem at all.'

CHAPTER TWELVE

Step 12: Add a Platter of Sweet Dreams

'Is IT safe to come in yet?'

'No. You are still in disgrace.' Sienna fluttered her hands in front of her face to wave him away. 'Go talk to the boys who are loading the skip with rancid carpet and broken furniture while the rain holds off.'

'I did explain on the way back that Jess is Chris's only daughter. How could I let Jess down when her party venue was flooded out? You only have a sixth birthday once in your life. That's special!'

'You are wasting your time looking at me with those pleading eyes,' Sienna said as she pressed tape onto the back of a picture frame.

She raised the scissors and waved the pointy ends at him before he had a chance to reply.

'*How could you do this to me?* How could you promise a little girl a fabulous birthday party when we don't even have a room to eat in? Three days, Brett. Two for the paint to be dry. There is so much to do it is making my head spin!'

The scissors were put to use on the tape and she added the framed photograph to the stack by her side. 'I am onto your cunning plan now,' she added with a shake of the head. 'You have those male-model good looks and the kind of winning smile that makes girls go dizzy, and then you go and spoil it all by agreeing to things without asking me first.'

Brett grinned at her and leant both of his elbows on the table, so that he could stare into her face with an innocent look. 'Do I make *you* go dizzy?'

Sienna picked up the next photograph and moved the mounting card around until she had the best frame for her Great-Uncle Louis. She fought down the temptation to groan out loud when the memory of the magical ten minutes she had spent with Brett on the basement steps tingled through her body. Dizzy did not come close.

'You did for a few seconds before you went crazy and started making promises without knowing all of the facts,' she replied, when photo and card were lined up. Then her hands stilled. She *was* talking about Brett now, wasn't she? *Not Angelo?*

She shrugged off the idea and carried on.

'Now I can put the dizziness down to low blood sugar and lack of sleep. Could happen to anyone. Lucky for me that Henry's niece is running his fish-and-chip shop while he and my aunt are sunning themselves in Spain. I popped in to say hello and catch up with the gossip on the way back from the flooring shop. Maria is on the mend, Henry is thinking of opening a café on the beach in Benidorm, and I think his niece has succumbed to your dizziness because she offered me free chips if I sent you in… What?'

Brett had started groaning and dropped his head forward to his chest.

'Maria!' He sighed. 'I *knew* there was something I had forgotten to do this morning. Call Maria and let her know how things were going. I know that woman. She will be driving the nurses mad if she is out of the loop and can't control everything, and—'

His head came up, and whatever he was thinking hit Brett so fast and so hard it was like a blow which knocked him backwards and ended up with him slapping the palm of his hand flat on Maria's dining-room table.

'Oh, that is *brilliant*!' he said, shaking his head from side to side.

'An undeniable truth, but what have I just missed?'

His answer was to casually stroll over, take hold of both her upper arms and physically take her weight while he pressed warm full lips to her cheek.

The intense scent of Brett filled Sienna's senses with delight, and cooking, and Brett.

Blue eyes focused intently on hers and his voice was calm, determined, with only the glint in his eyes giving the game away.

'You are a beautiful, clever woman—and I am sorry that I did not ask you first before I offered Chris the use of the bistro. I am an idiot. Maria Rossi is a genius. You are a princess. I am begging you to give me a *second* second chance. Won't happen again.'

Then he let go of her arms, so that she dropped back a couple of inches onto her low heels in a stunned daze.

'You're doing it again with the dizzy thing. Please explain what strange thoughts are going through that head of yours.'

'I've simply remembered something Maria said to me on the phone the other day. About you being a typical Rossi. Chip off the old block. There is a lot more of Maria in you than you care to admit. Right down to being a bit of a control freak! That's all. Give me another chance. You know that you want to.' And he flashed her the cheekiest wink she had ever seen.

'Do I indeed? Maybe I should have eaten those free chips after all? Because that makes no sense whatsoever. You have to be the world's best at making my poor brain spin. Take a paper prize. And, yes, okay—one more chance. *One*. Third time and you are out on your ear.'

He laughed. 'Thank you. I love prizes. And here's one for you. I actually came in to tell you that Chris will be here with the gang, bright and early tomorrow morning, to start taking out the big window. Those boys will need some real food in exchange for all of the work I have lined up, and chips are not on the menu. Not in our kitchen.'

Her head came up. '*Our* kitchen? Umm. *Much better*. In that case, Chef Cameron, I should warn you that any minute now two hunky blokes will be laying a new wooden floor, once the horrible smelly carpet has been ripped out.'

'Two-timing me already,' he muttered with much tutting as he planted both hands on his hips. 'No other way you could persuade tradesmen to turn up at such short notice.'

She couldn't help it. She had to press her lips together hard to stop herself grinning.

'Simple. I told them it was for Maria. They were round like a shot, offered me a big discount on a lovely new oak floor and agreed to fit it today. Apparently the boards click together like a jigsaw puzzle. Very clever. Our dining room is going to look superb.'

'*Our* dining room? Like the sound of that. Umm. *Much better*, Miss Rossi.'

And just like that the invisible cord that tied them together was pulled so taut she was frightened it was going to knock her over onto the table and into his arms if she didn't lean backwards slightly.

His eyes softened, the pupils wide and alert. He was feeling it too, and her poor broken heart missed a beat.

This time it was not the sound of music which snapped the cord, but doorbells. And hammering.

'Front door. Flooring,' she said, without breaking eye contact.

'Back door. Dishwasher,' he replied, with the kind of infectious grin that made it impossible for her not to surrender to the smile that had been bursting to come out since he'd planted that kiss on her cheek. 'Later.'

And he turned and was gone.

Sienna stared in silence at the space where he had just been standing. It was impossible to stay annoyed with this man! Drat him for having the most infectious grin! When in the past twelve years had he picked up *that* unique skill? And talk about stubborn!

Strange how much she was coming to like it.

CHAPTER THIRTEEN

Step 13: And Three Wedding Cakes...

'BIRTHDAY cake. Has to be pink, of course. Jess is totally into pink at the moment. Even her pencil case and school bag have to be pink. Apparently it's driving her nanny around the bend.'

'Pink ice cream. Pink jelly. Pink cake. Got it. Do we have pink birthday cake candles?'

'Absolutely. I have already told Chris that pink pizza is out—it's do-able, but you wouldn't want to eat it. Too much food colouring.'

Sienna paused in taking notes long enough to shudder. 'Yuk. Her mother is going to freak. Can you imagine eight little girls high on sugar and artificial colours? Do you have to check the ingredients with her first?'

'Her mother? Ah. Of course. You wouldn't know about Lili,' Brett whispered.

He leant further inside their replacement dish-washer and scrubbed the stainless steel as though there was some form of pestilence living there, and as if he had not already cleaned every surface until it shone, inside and out.

'Lili? Is that Jessica's mum?'

A quick intake of breath.

'Was. Lili died of cancer when Jess was four. Chris has been on his own since then.'

Sienna put down her pen and paper and her shoulders slumped. 'Oh, that's tragic. How terrible. Did you know her well?'

There was just enough of a pause for Sienna to stretch to one side, so that she could see the rear end of Brett as he moved on the dishwasher. Several years of frustrated hormones and deliberate celibacy counted for nothing when she had *that* view to look at. Could those denims *be* any tighter?

He was dirty, scraped with rust and rainwater from manhandling two dishwashers in and out of the kitchen in the dusk of a winter evening, and the hem of his T-shirt was soaked with washing water—but he was still the best-looking man she had seen in a very long time.

And he had been working harder than any head chef she had ever worked with—including her own dad. Angelo had never cleaned and scrubbed in his life. There had always been someone lower down the food chain to do it for him. Not Brett. She admired him for that—and he had stuck to his word. Their new dishwasher was a huge improvement.

Then that fine rear shuffled back, and he stretched up to his full height, rolling his shoulders back to release the tension and restore some flexibility, and giving her the benefit of a flash of exposed skin above his belt as the T-shirt rose higher, stretching taut across his chest.

She swung back in an instant, heat flashing at her throat.

'Sorry—did you ask me a question just then? The rack got stuck.'

I'll say!

'I was just wondering how you came to know Chris and his family,' she replied, trying to keep a casual tone in her voice now that he was within touching distance.

The salty tang of masculine sweat, antiperspirant and cleaning spray filled the space. No expensive perfume could have been so enticing. She lifted her chin and smiled.

'Curiosity. Being nosy. You can tell me to mind my own business if you like.'

Brett wandered over towards her and dried his hands, before collapsing down on a bar stool with a bottle of water.

'Not at all. But I have a question for you first. Do you have a best friend? Someone you can talk to any time, day or night, about anything?'

Sienna tried not to stare at the gleam of sweat on his throat as he swallowed down the cold water, or the wet curls of dark blond hair that extended down inside the shirt.

'As a matter of fact I do,' she gushed. 'Carla is the head receptionist at Greystone. We met on our first day at college. She is a real character! Why do you ask?'

Brett nodded and drained the water. 'Ten years ago I hit Paris, with the address of a restaurant I had never seen in my life on a scrap of paper, about four words of French, and no social skills whatsoever. But I had a fire in my belly and I was prepared to put up with the ribbing from the French guys to make my way.'

He held up one hand. 'There was one other English guy in the whole place. Chris. Oh, I do beg your pardon. The Honourable Christopher Donald Hampton Fraser.'

Brett stood to attention and bowed towards the dishwasher.

'Chris had come straight out of a fancy business school, had several degrees under his belt, and was being fast-tracked to great things with a hotel chain who owned the kitchen. A big one. Some wag at the restaurant decided it would be fun to cram the scruffy, sullen galley slave into the same tiny flat with the elegant smooth guy who spoke perfect French and watch the fireworks.'

Brett grinned and pressed two fingers to his forehead in a silent salute.

'Best two years of our lives. I never worked so hard in my life—or had so much fun.'

Sienna caught his infectious grin and smiled back at him.

'So you didn't kill each other after all?'

'Oh, I wanted to. Especially after he binned all my clothes and then cut my ponytail off when I was asleep.'

Her mouth fell forward with a gasp. 'He did not!'

'A Cameron and a Fraser in the same room! Both born in Scotland! Bound to be trouble—for all of five minutes.'

He leant forward to rest his elbows on his knees, hands cradling the empty water bottle, at just enough of an angle so that Sienna could see further down the front of his moistened T-shirt.

'Chris grabbed me on my first night off, when all I wanted to do was sleep, and forced me to share several bottles of very good wine. Hours later we decided that I was a young, scruffy and ignorant poor mess, he was an older, wiser and richer mess, and together we were going to conquer the world.'

Brett raised his bottle of water in a toast. 'Watch out, world! Here we come!'

They laughed out loud at the same time, Sienna shaking her shoulders in delight at the image.

'So what happened after you pledged world domination. Was there a master scheme?'

'Oh, yes. I was going to become a charismatic celebrity chef who would woo the customers, while good old Chris would run the business side and count the cash. It was brilliant. Except for one tiny, tiny detail.'

She looked up and raised her eyebrows with a little shake of the head, as if to say *carry on*.

'I wasn't charismatic. I was quiet, withdrawn, bitter and angry at the world, and I had zero confidence in myself and my talent. And I had dyslexia. Apart from those small problems we couldn't lose!'

'What changed? How did you do it? I mean, Chef in a Kilt? Excuse me for being so bold, but that is *not* the persona of a galley slave without an ounce of confidence!'

Brett winced and bared his teeth. 'Saw that, did you? Did I mention that Chris is also my manager and publicist? He's the only man alive who could persuade me to don the Cameron tartan!'

'Manager… Publicist…' Sienna nodded sagely. 'Aha. I think my point is proven. Hunk of the Month was a *very* popular feature at Greystone Manor.'

There was a gruff clearing of the throat from the man in the chair. 'Is that really what they called me?'

She nodded slowly, just once, and took delicious pleasure in seeing Brett groan, blink hard, and squirm in embarrassment before she smiled and took the edge off his pain.

'You're a lot braver than I am. Should I be asking Chris to give me some tips on how best to win friends and influence people?'

'Easy. The same way that I persuaded him into investing his hard-earned savings in a joint venture. Namely that special restaurant that we dreamt up in Paris all those years ago, as some kind of crazy wine-fuelled dream. Well, that dream will be opening in a few weeks. One thing was for sure. When I got tired of working as head chef for other people, Chris wasn't the *first* person I called. He was the *only* person I called.'

'Trust. There's a lot of trust there.'

'Both ways,' he admitted with a wink. 'I've sold everything I had in Adelaide to make my investment in the site. He's a single parent who's backing his shirt on this new place. We're both taking a huge risk.'

'But you still haven't answered my question. How did you go from galley slave in Paris—' and she waved her arm towards the darkness outside the kitchen window '—to Hunk of the Month who's about to open his own place?'

Brett leant forward to rest his elbows on his knees and prop his chin up with his hands, and for a moment he had all of the vulnerability of the teenage Brett that she remembered. Her heart leaped.

'I was in Paris. I was single. And I was doing the job I loved to the exclusion of everything else in my life. I didn't go out. I worked twenty-hour shifts. It was mad, but it was all I knew. Chris was the one who introduced me to the wonderful city and a world outside the kitchen that I had no idea existed. He made me talk to people. Talk to *girls!*'

Brett screwed up his face into a look of mock terror and shuddered, which made them both smile.

'I found out who I was in Paris, and eventually I was ready to take the final step and actually ask a specific girl for a date.'

He paused and gave Sienna a poignant smile. Not a full-mouthed grin but something quite different.

Something deeply personal.

He was going to tell her something it would cost him to admit.

Something worth her silence.

He leant back for a moment, to select a perfect strawberry from the bowl on the worktop.

'Lili was a Parisian girl, right down to her manicure and perfect skin. She was clever, polished, elegant, and so beautiful it took your breath way. The kind of girl that every other woman envies and every man wants to have on his arm.'

Sienna's eyes never left his face as Brett held the strawberry by its stalk and took a delicate bite from the juicy fruit. The tang and sweetness of the berry hit her nose with sensory overload.

But she stayed silent.

This was a story that only Brett could tell, and he swallowed down the fruit, his gaze still fixed on the remains of the berry as he spoke.

'I had waited eighteen months to ask her out for a drink on a double date with Chris and his girl-friend. I had hoped and dreamt that she would say yes. But it still came as a shock when she agreed. For a few hours I was the happiest man in Paris. Until the moment Lili laid eyes on my pal Chris. Love at first sight for both of them. Poor fool didn't know what had hit him.'

Brett popped the rest of the strawberry into his mouth and pulled out the stalk and hull in one piece.

'Four months later I stood next to Chris as his best man when he married Lili.'

The blunt statement was made without a hint of hesitation, but Sienna was close enough and focused enough to see the telltale twitch at the side of his mouth. His eyes narrowed and flinched so quickly that anyone else would have missed the signs which shouted out distress before he recovered and forced a light voice and a joky smile.

'I had to make three wedding cakes. *Three*. Five layers of light-as-a-feather sponge with fondant orchids for the British contingent. A tower of fresh profiteroles filled with Chantilly cream served with warm chocolate sauce for her French family and the kids. And of course a low-carb pink champagne jelly with fresh fruit for the fashion models who—'

He never got the final words out, because Sienna couldn't bear to tolerate the deep, deep pain in his voice any longer. and before he could finish the sentence she crossed the few feet that separated them, leant in, and covered his lips with hers.

She tasted the salty tang of his sweat, and the sweet strawberry juice in the heat of his mouth, and he froze for a moment. Then he kissed her back, sweet, welcoming, insistent, blanking out any coherent thought that might have lingered in her brain.

Eyes closed, she felt the soft warmth and taste and scent of his kiss wash over her like a warm blanket, drowning her in the sensation of being held in the circle of his arms, so that when he finally pulled away, her head fell forward onto his chest.

Heat. His unique body fragrance. The background of light jazz music playing on the radio. Her senses reeled with the intensity of the moment.

She was going to capture this in her memory. Savour every second.

Instantly his hand moved to the back of her head, and she became aware of the vague pressure of his lips on the top of her hair as he held her closer.

Her hands pressed hard on his damp chest, the thumping heat of his heartbeat resonated though her fingers, telling her everything she needed to know about the man. Her instincts were right, even if she was not ready to open her eyes and look at him.

No. She wasn't ready for that. Not yet.

His hand caressed the back of her head, and the heat of his forehead pressed against her hair, made her tremble. His voice was low, and so close to her ear that it was more of a whisper. 'What did I do to deserve that?'

'Does there have to be a reason?' she answered, her words muffled into his chest.

His hand slid down her back from her hairline, and she could almost feel the mental and physical barriers coming down between them as he pulled back and lifted her chin so that he could look at her.

The look brought tears to her eyes. Intensity. Confusion. Pain. It was all there.

'No pity. Lili chose the better man.'

Don't say that. Don't ever say that. You deserve better than to feel that way!

She swallowed down the fast response and stroked the line of his jaw with one finger, still not ready to look into those laser blue eyes where she knew she would instantly be lost.

Whatever happened between them going forward, the very *last* thing she wanted was for Brett to think that she had kissed him out of some sense of pity!

Yes, she did feel sorry for him.

Brett had been in love with Lili. Who had married his best friend.

He had lost the woman he had loved not just once, but twice.

First to his best friend and then to disease. But *her* feelings for him were *way* more complicated than that, and they both deserved better.

If Brett believed that he was a lesser man than Chris, then perhaps she could do something creative to redress that balance.

Starting right now.

'Then how about understanding? I *am* sorry for your loss. And,' she replied with a warm smile, 'little Jess is going to have the best birthday party *ever!*'

The tension eased from his shoulders and his chest dropped a few inches under her hands.

'Okay…' Then a second small smile of mutual understanding crept over his face before he repeated, 'Okay…' But this time it was in a stronger voice as he fought to regain control.

His arms moved away from her waist and rubbed up and down her arms for a few seconds as his breathing slowed.

She gave him one long smile, and then slapped the palms of her hands twice against his T-shirt before stepping out of the circle of his arms and casually picking up her clipboard.

'Pink balloons. Let's make that thirty. A girl can never have too many pink balloons, and each of the guests can have one to take home.'

She risked a faint smile in his direction, and was rewarded with a grin and a tip of the head.

'Absolutely! In the meantime I'm heading for the shower. Then how about we pay a visit to the local pizza shop? Check out the competition! Especially when you still have to practise your singing and pizza-making skills.'

'You're on. Except I can't cook and I don't sing. Apart from those two tiny details, I'm starving! Then we need to get seriously busy to make that room ready for a *real* little princess. I'm only a pretend one, after all.'

The scent of strawberry still lingered and wrapped around her senses as he strolled out of the kitchen, so casually it was hard to believe that he had just turned her world upside down.

Time to turn up the heat.

She had meant what she said.

Lili's daughter was going to celebrate her birthday in a lovely room—even if she had to work all night to finish the paintwork.

Except she had the strange feeling that she would be doing it more for Brett than the little girl whose mother had broken his heart.

Brett was a better man than he knew. And she was the one who was going to show him just how special he truly was. Even if it meant kissing him again to prove it!

CHAPTER FOURTEEN

Step 14: Eight Spinning Designer
Rainbow Pizzas...

BRETT STOOD in the middle of the dining room, pushed his hands deep into his trouser pockets and gave a low whistle.

This was his first official viewing of the redecorated room. And it took his breath away.

Sienna had chosen a warm natural oak wood flooring which worked brilliantly against the fresh cream paintwork. The tablecloths, napkins, curtains and lampshades were plain forest green or pastel pink, with a faint check in the same colours as a border.

Even on a cool February afternoon light flooded into the room through the pristine window glass, increasing the sense of space and relaxed comfort.

All in all, the overall impression was modern, chic, clean—but also comfortable and welcoming.

This was not Maria Rossi's trattoria any more. This was Sienna Rossi's bistro.

Everything about this room screamed Sienna. Her personal style shone through in all the details his trained eye picked up around the room.

The family photos were in plain oak picture frames which perfectly matched the floorboards and the chair backs. But it was the arrangement that was so clever.

Sienna had collected them into groups of four, all hung on one wall—the far wall—so that they would be the first thing the customers saw when they came into the dining room from the street. The eye was immediately drawn to the smiling faces of the Rossi family who had gone before, in order for her to be in this world.

But it was the long, plain dining-room wall which was so amazing that he could only stand and smile at what she had achieved.

The words *Trattoria Rossi* had been painted in forest green in large letters along the whole of the middle section, using the same type of script Sienna had chosen for their new plate-glass window. He would never have thought of using the same stencil that had been used by the glaziers on the outside inside the room. The same name, inside and outside. Fresh green inside, acid etch outside.

It was inspired.

Put that together with sparkling glassware and simple but elegant cutlery, and he was looking at the idealised perfect yet informal dining area he had searched for all of his life.

He had never told Sienna what his dream was, never described it or even mentioned it. Yet this amazing, wonderful, special woman had created the dining room he had been talking to Chris about ever since Paris.

There were already *way* too many formal restaurants, where starchy people in smart uncomfortable clothes were served wonderful, spectacular showpiece dishes made by master craftsmen at the top of their game. Meals were usually eaten in silence, or with classical music played in hushed tones in the background, and children were considered an unnecessary nuisance to be tolerated.

He had worked in hotels and restaurants all over the world that specialised in providing an exclusive experience to the privileged few who could afford the cost of total luxury.

Of course they were brilliant! And he had loved working for those masters of their craft. But that was not what he wanted for his own restaurant. Far from it.

His dream was to serve fantastic food cooked with love in precisely the same type of warm, open, friendly and informal surroundings he had seen in the Rossi family home all those years ago and experienced for himself in family restaurants across Europe.

Whichever country he had visited, for work or holiday, he had made it his business to ask the local people where *they* would recommend for a family meal. Friendly, open and welcoming dining rooms, where whole generations of families could come together to celebrate good food.

He had sought out dining rooms where guests of all ages, all sizes and all shapes were equally welcome. Where they could relax and be comfortable. Free to laugh and argue and sing and dance if they wanted.

All the time searching for his ideal version of a family restaurant, where children would be welcome and the whole family could eat wonderful food at the same table.

That was why Chris had searched all over London to find the perfect location where there would be enough space to accommodate children, laughter and music while he created the food to match.

The irony was that he had found it in the very place where he had started his career all those years ago!

There were footsteps on the hard oak floorboards.

Sienna came to stand next to him, and he could sense her anxiety seeping out of every pore of her skin. A quick glance sideways told him what he needed. She was chewing the corner of her mouth with her top teeth.

The great Sienna Rossi, princess of the Rossi clan, was nervous in case he hated the room she had worked so hard to create, and wanted it turned back to terracotta dark walls and gloomy spider lairs before Jess arrived for her party.

Without thinking or hesitating, he reached out and took her hand in his, meshing their fingers together so that they stood in silence together and looked around the space.

It smelt of fresh paint and wood varnish.

And as far as he was concerned it was magical.

'I only had time for one more coat of paint last night, but it is dry. Jessica and her friends will be fine today, and then I'll clear the walls and finish off over the weekend.'

'You don't need to change a thing. It's perfect.'

'Really?'

'*Really* really. It's everything I could wish for. And more. Maria is going to be delighted.'

He lifted his chin a little and focused on the brass rail holding up the bistro curtain as he squeezed her fingers.

'I love it.' *I love you.*

He was conscious of his breathing speeding up to match hers, and the gentle pressure of her fingertips as they pressed against his in return.

For a few precious minutes they were not Brett Cameron and Sienna Rossi, with all the baggage those names carried with them, but two people who wanted to be with one another and had worked their whole lives so that they could stand side by side in *this* room at *this* moment in time.

He would not have missed it for the world.

Brett glanced at her from the corner of his eye and his stomach clenched. She was exasperating, stubborn and awkward—and absolutely gorgeous.

Words formed in his mouth, and he was just about to tell her how pretty she looked that morning when there was a bustle of activity and balloons from the hallway and Sienna dropped his hand as though it was burning.

'Did someone place an order for pink balloons?' Chris asked, his fingers clamped around enough balloons for him to be grateful that he carried his own gravity around with him.

Like a guilty teenager caught in a clinch, Brett shuffled as far from Sienna as he could without being insulting, and pretended to be testing that the wall lights worked.

As nonchalantly as he could manage, Brett turned to his friend just in time to see Sienna fling her arms around Chris's neck and kiss him heartily on the cheek.

'Chris. You are a genius. Thank you, thank you, and thank you. You've done an amazing job. The window is fantastic!'

Considering that she had only met Chris once before, when he'd introduced the glaziers, this was a little over the top!

'Hey! I'm right here,' Brett intervened, pointing to his chest. 'And I seem to remember *I* was the one who has fed and watererd six workmen every hour on the hour for most of the day. Don't I get a hug?'

'Chance would be a fine thing.'

She turned back to Chris, who was looking at Brett with thinly veiled superiority and amusement.

'It's so sad when he grovels,' she said. 'Are you bringing Jess later? I can't wait to meet her!'

'My slave driver of a business partner needs me to work on this signature restaurant of his—' he scowled at Brett, who simply shrugged his shoulders '—but I'll be here for the cake bit, and to pick her up.' His eye caught Brett's with a wink. 'Something tells me that my little girl is going to have a whale of a time with you two around.'

'Is there anyone here who likes pizza?'

Every single girl in the room put her hand up. Including three of the nannies and Sienna.

'Excellent. Well, in that case, today we are making...*pizza!*'

Sienna smiled as the room exploded with cheers and waving, and even a pirouette from the twins in identical ballet shoes and pink tutus.

'But not just any old pizza. Oh, no. Today we are making Jessica's special rainbow pizza. *And...* each person gets to choose their very own, special, unique, personal and only for them rainbow, which only they get to eat!'

'Pizza!' Jess called out, and waved her pink sparkly wand in the air while jumping up and down in her very pretty matching outfit, pink from hair to slippers.

'Rainbow pizza. Rainbow pizza!' they all called

out, waving their fairy wands so vigorously that Brett had to reach forward and straighten Jess's tiara, which had fallen forward onto her face.

He stretched up onto the toes of his training shoes and put the flat of his hand to the front of his forehead like a cap, eyes screwed up in concentration as he turned from side to side from the waist.

'Where *did* I put those big pizza plates? Has anyone seen the big pizza plates? We can't make pizzas without pizza plates.'

There were giggles from behind the wands as Brett put both hands on his hips in his best sea captain impression and pointed directly at Sienna, who shuffled from side to side, whistling and looking at the ceiling—which was a big mistake, because hiding behind the light shade was a damp patch she had not noticed before—pretending to hide a stack of metal pizza plates behind her back.

'There they are. Aunty Sienna is hiding them! Aren't you, Aunty Sienna? *Naughty* Aunty Sienna.'

Brett wiggled his eyebrows at her and grinned.

He had every right to look victorious. There was no other man in the world who could have persuaded her to wear one of her aunt Maria's girly-pink flouncy dresses, cinched around the waist with a huge pink ribbon tied in a big bow at the side.

Especially when Maria was a good four inches shorter, which made for a lot more exposure of her legs above the knee than she was used to. A *lot* more.

No wonder he was enjoying the view.

'Now, dig your fingers in there. That's it. Stretch it out nice and round. Push into the corners, just like that—see what I'm doing?'

'Katie, sweetie, that's looking a bit square. Stretch it out. Like this—there you go. No, it doesn't matter if your nail varnish goes into it.'

'Wait. What's that music? Can you hear that music? What does the music tell us to do? *Mambo*!'

The kids all bellowed out the tune, since this was the twentieth time they had heard it, swaying and dancing from side to side, and Sienna could not resist joining in with the chorus, which made Brett look up and smile.

'Hey, I knew you had a lovely singing voice inside there! Let's all sing like Aunty Sienna. That's it, Jess, mambo.'

'Now we have to do the dance. Are you all ready? Let's spin that pizza to the music!'

Brett wiggled his bottom from side to side and made his shoulders do a little dance as he turned the dough round and pushed, then turned it again before looking up and dramatically staring around the table.

'Oh, *look* at these fantastic pizzas! One more dance, and then all they need are the magic words!'

Brushing the flour from his hands, he went around the table from child to child, whispering something secret in each ear which made the girls squirm and giggle.

'How does the magic work, Uncle Brett?'

Brett stepped back and looked hard at Jess.

'You mean, you've never seen it?'

She shook her head and looked around at her pals, and they shook their heads and shrugged.

'Well, that is just terrible. Does anyone else want to see the magic?'

Frantic nodding ensued.

'Okay. Here we go. Have to get ready first. Loosen up the old fingers.'

Brett stretched his hands out and wiggled his fingertips up and down on both hands, sprinkling flour everywhere as he did so. Eight little girls did the same, waving their hands in the air, some still clutching the pink plastic wands which Sienna noticed had lost a lot of their glitter. Probably into the pizza dough.

'Oh, that *is* better. You need both hands for

this job. Ready everyone? I can feel that magic. Here it comes!'

Before they could answer, Brett flipped up his own piece of pizza dough and twirled it into the air, spinning it into a circle before passing it to his other hand so quickly that it was a blur.

Sienna watched the children stare open mouthed as Brett flicked his wrist and the circle of pizza lifted up into the air again, spun slightly, and fell back into his upraised hands. He slapped it down on the floured board.

'*Wooow*! That was so cool. Do it again, Uncle Brett. Do it again.'

'Yes, do it again, Uncle Brett.' Sienna smiled across at him in between helping the nannies—who were all ogling Brett—with refastening aprons and picking up fairy wings and wands which had lost their charm compared to Uncle Brett. Not that she blamed them. He was…wonderful.

The love shone through every time he looked at the children. He *adored* them. Being with them, talking to them, sharing their fun. He was one of them.

'For the pretty lady—anything!' He smiled back. 'You see, there are some advantages from starting your catering career in a takeaway pizza parlour on an industrial estate. I could spin sixty a night before I turned sixteen.'

Sienna nodded at the children, who were still entranced by his hands as he draped the dough and then spun it higher and higher, before catching it one-handed and slapping it back to the table.

'Yay! Do it again, Uncle Brett—do it again!'

She nodded more fiercely this time, and he got the message. 'Of course university is much better. But you can always do this for fun at weekends! What do you say? Are you all ready to make magic spinning pizzas?'

'Yes!'

As each of the children lifted and flung their dough shapes around the room, Brett bent down to Jess and lifted her up into his arms, twirling her from side to side to the music, sharing in her childish laughter before she threw her arms around his neck and kissed him on the cheek.

A lightbulb switched on inside Sienna's head.

And her heart broke.

Jess was all Brett had left of the woman he had loved in Paris. She was so pretty, so delicate and dainty and happily unspoilt. Her mother, Lili, must have been a remarkable woman.

All she could do was watch them as they danced and sang together.

The tall, god-handsome blond man, who had always owned her heart from the moment she had seen him as a teenager, and the little girl in a pink tutu.

If ever there was a man who wanted his own family, she was looking at him now.

He had let down his guard, and the loving, caring and oh-so-vulnerable side of the real Brett shone through. And pulled her closer to him than she'd ever thought possible.

He had so many special gifts! She already knew that he could be tender and compassionate. The thought of him going through life alone was so terrible that hot tears pricked the back of her eyes, startling her with their intensity.

Was it possible that Brett could ever open his generous and warm heart to take a chance on love again? With her?

She was falling in love with Brett Cameron all over again, and there was not one thing she could do about it except run away before they broke each other's hearts.

She needed to get back to Greystone Manor. Back to the stone walls and safe places where she would only have to cope with awkward diners—not a handsome and loving blond man who adored children and would make a wonderful father.

CHAPTER FIFTEEN

Step 15: And Two Glasses of Red Wine

THREE HOURS later, the dining room was re-markably quiet and almost calm. The party was over and the clean-up crew had swung into action.

That was to say Brett had worked his magic with their new dishwasher, and Sienna was repairing the damage to her newly painted room. Her frilly dress was gone, replaced with comfy trousers, a waterproof apron and a pair of loafers she'd last worn when she was at college.

Every child had been stuffed to bursting with pizza topped with ingredients they had chosen themselves—she was the only person who had noticed that Brett had discreetly picked off several pieces of banana before dramatically sliding them into the oven with a great flourish.

He was a natural showman. No doubt about it.

And he certainly had a way with the girls. But the pizzas had looked and smelled delicious when he'd slowly drawn them out, golden and bubbling, to the accompaniment of 'oohs' and 'aahs' from their designers.

She had rarely seen food enjoyed with so much delight and enthusiasm. The pizzas had gone down even faster than the ice cream, raspberry sauce and gorgeous fruit jelly.

The young ladies and more than a few nannies had then been served pink fizzy lemonade in plastic champagne glasses to wash down the heavenly light pink birthday cake. And Brett had been called into service to hold Jess up while she blew out the birthday candles with her father Chris by her side.

Overall it had been a fabulous party. And well worth all the effort.

Shame that there was always pain associated with gain.

Sienna stretched up on tiptoe to wipe away two tiny pieces of pizza dough which had stuck to the dining-room ceiling after the extra-vigorous tossing practice.

'You wouldn't think that a six year old would have so much strength in her wrist. Watch out, world. Here they come. I'm frightened already. I wonder if I was so precocious at that age.'

Brett replied with a snort, then wiped his hands on the kitchen towel around his waist and carefully pulled the cork on one of the bottles of wine that Chris had deposited in exchange for a carload of squealing young ladies in sparkly pink sandals, clutching goody bags and balloons.

'Jess is a total sweetheart. I can see how she twists all the men in her life around her little finger. Especially her uncle Brett. She's a little diva in the making. No doubt about it.' She stretched higher, but still could not reach the floury patch.

'Here. Let me do that for you.'

Brett stood behind her and pressed his front into her back as he reached up with a wet sponge to wipe away a smear of sticky dough—only then he found another, and another. Any excuse for their bodies to be in contact for as long as possible.

She turned around and gave him a look. 'Thank you, but I think we are done. Time to call it a day.'

Her response was met with a chuckle, but he did concede and sat down at one of the dining-room tables. 'Amen to that. Ready for some supper? I have a very nice platter of antipasti from Frank's Deli, and a vintage Sangiovese from that grower near Pisa that Chris seems to like. And there's always more birthday cake if you need the sugar!'

Sienna groaned and pressed her hand to her stomach as she put away her cleaning materials and untied her apron. 'Thank you, but I'll stick to the antipasti. I was the one who had to share in six table picnics! It's so embarrassing when you can't manage to eat the same amount of pink cake as a six year old.'

Brett very carefully poured a tasting sample of the wine into two large wineglasses.

'Well, I hope this wine goes some way to saying thank you. Chris would like to add it to our wine list in the new restaurant. You're the expert. I would welcome your opinion.'

'Modesty prevents me from bragging, but I do love matching food with wine.'

Brett sat back in the new dining-room chair, legs stretched out under the table, and watched Sienna as she swirled the wine in the glass, her nose deep inside the wide bowl, sighing in appreciation before taking a tiny sip.

Delicate fingers selected a choice sliver of salty Parma ham and popped it into her mouth with pleasure, and a brief moan of delight that had fire-works lighting all over his body.

'That's good with the ham. Actually, I would go so far as to say that it's *very* good.' She lifted the glass towards him for a refill.

'Well, you certainly surprised me today, Miss Rossi.'

'Me, Chef Cameron?'

'You were brilliant! Truly! I always knew that head waiters went beyond the call of duty for their guests, but running a puppet show was a great idea.'

'Oh, it's amazing what you can do with paper napkins and a marker pen! You should try it some time—especially if you intend to run a family restaurant.'

'Which I do! Plus, someone who looked re-markably like you was singing. And for a moment you were actually making pizza with the kids. So tell me what else you don't do.'

'What do you mean?'

'Well, you told me that you don't sing and you can't cook. I was hoping that you would tell me that you never, ever go out with pizza chefs.'

Sienna put down her glass and leant slightly forward before saying, in a clear, low voice, 'I never, ever go out with chefs. Pizza or otherwise.'

There was just enough emotion in her voice for Brett to hold her gaze.

'I take it you have tried it and been burnt?'

'That's right.'

Brett opened his mouth to say something and then shook his head.

'Not André Michon from Greystone Manor? I mean, he's brilliant, and I wouldn't blame you, but…'

Sienna laughed out loud.

'No. I adore him—and so does his lovely wife. No. Definitely not André.'

Brett picked up the extra tension in the room when she was the first to break eye contact and focus instead on the glass of red wine which she was holding onto with both hands.

'I'm surprised that Maria didn't keep you up to date with the gossip on my past love-life.' Her eyes flicked up and saw his confusion. 'Obviously not. The truth is that I was engaged to a chef a few years ago and it ended badly. So that's another reason for me to stay *out* of the kitchen and never, ever go out with pizza chefs.' She raised her glass and toasted Brett with a smile.

'He must have been quite someone. Would I know him?'

She faltered for a few seconds before replying as casually as she could, with a slight nod. 'You might do. It's no secret, and someone is bound to tell you. Does the name Angelo Peruzi ring any bells?'

There was a stunned silence for a few seconds before he replied in a low voice, 'You were engaged to *Angelo Peruzi?*'

'And he was engaged to me. Only he seemed to forget that fact when he moved back to Los Angeles.'

Brett blew out hard and raised his glass towards her. 'Peruzi. I met him at an award ceremony in Milan. Like I say, you are certainly full of surprises. He's a lucky man. I'm sorry it didn't work out.'

She popped a stuffed olive into her mouth and played with some bread for far longer than necessary before answering.

'So am I. And, yes, he *was* a lucky man. Long gone. Or should I say he *was* long gone? The wine is brilliant with the bread but a disaster with the olives. Sorry.'

Brett took a sip of the wine and winced.

'Right again. The wine stays. The olives are out. And you are changing the subject. Do you mean that Peruzi is back in London? I haven't heard anything about that.'

'Then here is a piece of juicy gossip hot off the press. You already know that André Michon is retiring at the end of the month. Well, come March

Angelo Peruzi is going to be the new head chef at Greystone Manor. He is definitely back! It was officially announced yesterday, so I think I have a few days' grace before my friends start calling to find out what's going on.'

Brett pursed his lips together. 'How do you feel about working with him again? Isn't that going to be a little awkward? Or do you think you will get back together again?'

'Back with Angelo? No. Never,' Sienna replied in a dark voice, with a firm shake of her head. 'And *awkward* does not come close. But the truth is I don't have many options. I *have* to go back to Greystone.'

She looked around the room before turning back to him with a smile. 'This has been fun, and I want to help Maria as much as I can, but I have responsibilities. People are relying on me. I have worked so hard to be promoted to restaurant manager; I really can't afford to miss the opportunity.'

Brett reached out and wrapped his long fingers around her hand so tenderly that the touch of his fingertips on the back of her hand took her by surprise.

'Congratulations on your promotion. But there are always options. Other jobs.' His head lifted. 'Here is an idea. Why don't you come and work for me? I don't have a head waiter or a sommelier. Actually, I don't have *any* staff at the minute! You can start with a clean slate. The entire Rossi family can visit and party any time they like—there's plenty of space. It would be great!'

He gave her one of those smiles designed to melt the heart of any woman within a hundred paces. And for a moment she was tempted. Very, very tempted. Except of course it would change nothing. She would spend the rest of her life waiting to be let down.

She reluctantly slid her hand away from his grasp as she gave him a thin smile.

'Thanks for the offer. And I really mean that. But it won't work. Why should I run away because my ex boyfriend is back in town? No, Brett. I can do my job. I lost my home and my career to Angelo once before. I'm not losing it again. I know it won't be easy, but I can do it. I won't let any man run my life for me again.'

Sienna turned away from him and gazed out through the new window towards the rooftops, where the light was already fading to dusk in the low winter sun.

Sienna straightened her back, suddenly conscious of the fact that she had said more about her personal life in the last few hours than in the past year. This was the first time she had actually said the words out loud.

But even scarier was the fact that Brett Cameron was sitting across the table from her. Watching her. Studying her.

'Would you mind if we change the subject? That's next week's challenge. Right now I just want to get through Valentine's Day! Here's a question for you. How did the young Brett Cameron come to meet my aunt Maria in the first place? I'm far more interested in hearing *that* story.'

Brett dropped his head back and howled with laughter.

'You mean, she didn't tell you?'

He stretched out his arms on the table as Sienna shook her head.

'I ate all her food! When I was nineteen, Maria came to my catering college to do a demonstration about yeast and pizza dough. Different shapes and sizes and what you can serve with them. That sort of thing. I was in trouble for fighting, and my punishment was to clear up after the cookery class.'

'Hold it there. You were *fighting*?' Her face screwed up in disbelief. 'I find that hard to believe.'

'Oh, believe it,' he replied with a nod. 'I had only

been there two months, and every one in my class took it in turns to come up with new insults for the stupid new guy who couldn't even read or write.'

He sighed out loud and grimaced. 'I won't repeat them. Just use your imagination. Believe me, it is no fun when you can't read. I was angry. Angry at my mum for moving—again! Perhaps if we'd stayed in one place someone might have spotted the problem and done something about it, instead of jumping to the easy conclusion that I was stupid, or lazy, and destined to follow my mum as a transient. Most of the time I think they were glad to see the back of me.'

'That must have been so hard. I'm sorry.'

'More frustrating than hard. I was angry at myself because I just couldn't work out what I was missing that the others found so easy! Angry at the teachers who were too stressed to ask why. And then one day a bully pushed me too far and I pushed back.'

She meshed the fingers of one hand between his and was rewarded with a smile.

He leant forward toward her. 'The thing Maria didn't know was that I had been working in the evenings at a pizza shop—my famous pizza spinning lessons—so when everyone had cleared out I picked up the leftover dough and ingredients and started making things with them. After half an hour I had a pretty decent foccacia on the table, and a couple of mini pizzas. My plan was to take them home for dinner, but I was so hungry that I started to eat them. Just as Maria came back.'

'Oh, no. What did she say?'

Brett grinned and shook his head. 'She said a lot. I ate. She asked questions. It didn't take her long to realise that I had memorised the recipes and had some talent. She offered me a job as a kitchen slave six nights a week and every weekend. Right here.'

He paused and looked around.

'Have you ever noticed that there are no cook-books in your aunt's kitchen? Not one. There are some in the house, but they are for show. Maria recognised that we shared something more than talent and a love of great food. She knew she had dyslexia, and had come up with her own ways of coping. She recognised the symptoms in me, and thought there was a good chance that I had dyslexia too.'

'Wow. My dad told me that she had dyslexia a few years ago, but I didn't really give it any thought. She's my aunt Maria and that's the only thing that matters.'

His fingers moved slowly over the surface of her hand, pressing out her fingers as he spoke with such devastating intensity that speech was not possible.

'She is also an amazingly stubborn lady. It took Maria three months to persuade me to be tested at a special unit. I didn't want to go and have more assessments! More tests and exams that I was bound to get wrong because I couldn't read. I was tired of being pigeonholed as an academic failure who was simply lazy and had to try harder. What a joke that was. As far as I was concerned it was one more way for the system to hang a label around my neck with the word *loser* on it.'

The pressure of his thumb on her knuckles had increased so much that Sienna almost cried out for fear of being bruised, but something stilled in his face as he looked into her eyes, and he released her with a brief smile.

'In the end it was the best thing that ever happened to me. Do you know I had never even heard the word *dyslexia* until the assessor told me what the tests were about? These tests were different. Patterns. Shapes. And logic. Not just words and sentences.'

Brett reached out for his wineglass and took a long sip before going on.

'I remember I was sitting outside the test room with Maria when the assessor came out and said that my scores were some of the highest he had ever seen. I was clever and visually gifted. Artistic and creative. And I had dyslexia. Not a severe case compared to some people, but enough to make a difference in most parts of my life where letters were concerned.'

He glanced up at her. 'Of course the first thing I thought was—oh, great, now the bullies get to call me mentally handicapped. Brilliant! But Maria made me sit and listen to what they could do to help make things easier at college. Like reading the recipes out before class. Using video and tapes. I could even record the lessons. Suddenly I saw I had a chance.' He chuckled. 'It was still tough. Especially at exam time. But Chris helped in Paris. And I have a better memory than most people. The rest, as they say, is history. So now you know. That's how I found out that I have dyslexia.'

He sat back now, and his shoulders seemed to drop a little.

'But, to look on the bright side, my lack of ability with printed words might have held back my academic studies, but it always felt so natural to cook, to create—I would have missed out on all that with a traditional education.'

Brett lifted his glass and smiled.

'Can I suggest a toast to the lovely Maria? Who taught me that sometimes it pays to be stubborn even when the rest of the world thinks you are worthless.'

'No. I'm going to raise my glass to both of you. You should be proud of what you have achieved. Thank you for being so honest. It means a lot.'

'You're welcome. To Maria!'

'Maria and Brett! Two of the most remarkable people I have ever met.'

She hadn't meant to say that. It had just come out. From the shocked look in Brett's eyes he'd been expecting it even less, and it took him a few seconds to recover.

'Thank you. And you're not so bad yourself. Restaurant Manager Rossi.'

With a sudden burst of energy, Brett stood up from the table and reached across to the worktop for birthday cake.

'Speaking of which, if I am so remarkable, perhaps I can persuade you to change your mind about my earlier offer?'

'Birthday cake?'

'If you like. Or working for me? Take your pick. Come on.' He bent down to her eye level and wafted the cake in front of her. 'You like Chris and Jess. We seem to get on all right. Come and work with me instead of at stuffy old Greystone Manor. You won't regret it.'

Sienna put down her glass very gently and stood up.

'Thanks, but no. To cake, *and* your job offer.'

Sienna stood in silence and watched one of the few men she had ever come this close to push his hands into his jean pockets, shoulders high to his neck with stress, his disappointment lingering like a bitter taste on the air.

He was so gentle and tender. So understanding.

She wanted to run to him. Hug him. Tell him that she would love to spend time with him in this enchanted place.

But that would mean trusting him with her happiness. Even for a few short days. Until he went one way and she another. And she couldn't do that. To either of them.

Because she could never trust another lover to also be her business partner. She knew now that love demanded absolute truth. In business, that same trust could kill you if the going got tough.

There was no future for her here, or in working with Brett.

Not now. Not ever.

CHAPTER SIXTEEN

Step 16: Smother in Wild Mushroom and Cream Sauce

SIENNA TURNED over and pulled the duvet a little closer around her shoulders as she snuggled down into the pillow and gave a little sigh of contentment.

Mmm. She was almost annoyed that she was being woken from such a sweet dream, in which Brett had carried her in his arms and laid her on a thick, warm bed.

Lovely.

She felt safe. This was such a comfy bed. Ultra-soft feather pillow. She could lie here all day.

Someone was knocking on her door, but she could afford to snuggle just a *little* longer. Birthday parties could be such hard work!

Her eyes creaked open. Just a little. Just to check the time. Strange that her alarm had not gone off. She stretched out her arm towards the bedside cabinet.

The alarm had not gone off because it was two thirty in the morning.

She pulled her arm back under the warm duvet and closed her eyes. For one complete millisecond. Before snapping them open and sitting up in the bed.

She collapsed back down again onto the pillows with a groan, and pulled the duvet over her head.

This was Maria's house, and something had woken her up in the middle of the night.

And the knocking had not gone away.

'Are you decent in there? I have coffee.'

She glanced down at her clothing before answering Brett. She was wearing her aunt's thick pink pajamas.

Yes, she was decent.

'Coffee would be good,' was her feeble reply, as she pushed herself up the bed and drew the covers up to cover her chest. *Pathetic. This was what happened when you agreed to work with chefs who assumed that you would be available twenty-four hours a day!*

'Have you any idea what time it is? It's the middle of the night! What are you doing knocking on my bedroom door at two in the morning? I should warn you that I have one of Maria's stiletto shoes and my brother's phone number if you try anything.'

Brett stopped pacing her bedroom for a few seconds to stare at her as though the problem was so obvious that she should have been able to work it out for herself.

'The three-mushroom sauce. It's not working. I've made it four times and it is still not working. I am going crazy.' He leant closer, so that their noses were almost touching. 'See these grey hairs? Crazy.'

'Mushroom sauce? Oh, thank goodness. Is that all?' Sienna replied as she collapsed back on the pillows.

'All? Oh, no, no. You don't understand. That is not *all*. Without the mushroom sauce I don't have wild-mushroom pasta, and we don't have anything to finish the braised organic chicken breast. Seriously, that chicken needs this sauce, and I am not going to bed until my recipe is perfect.'

Brett was pacing back and forward so rapidly that Sienna feared for the bedroom carpet. His own coffee was untouched, which was probably a good thing considering how much adrenaline must be rushing around his system.

He was obsessing about a sauce recipe.

Chefs. You either loved them or tolerated them, but either way you had to learn to live with them.

She covered her wide yawn with her hand before nodding between half closed eyes.

'Okay, I understand. Mushroom sauce. Got it. What can I do to help?'

'Thought you'd never ask. I need to borrow those amazing tastebuds of yours, because after four hours of this mine are fried. Tell me what you are about to eat. I want the fragrance of this sauce to tantalise your senses way before it hits, and then…'

'Then the flavour. I know. I can't guarantee that my tastebuds will be very responsive at this time of the morning, but I'll do what I can. Talk to me about the dish. What are the base notes?'

'Not this time. Tonight I want this sauce to do the talking for me. When those lovers taste this baby they will be putty in their partners' hands. So get ready to be blown away.'

'I'll be down in five minutes.'

Sienna sat down opposite Brett in the tiny kitchen and watched him fuss, stepping and reaching from pan to pan, dipping his tasting spoon into one then the other. Then grinding more black pepper and tasting again.

'Oh. Big talk from the big guy. So actually you are doing this for the boys, not the ladies? Is that right? Let me take a look in those pans. I'll soon tell you what I would be prepared to eat. *If* you can take the pressure?'

'Sorry. I want those girls looking at their dates, not the food.'

He reached forward and slid his bandana over Sienna's head, so that it rested on her forehead. 'Perfect. This test we are going to do blindfold.'

She lifted one hand to pull off the bandana, but he wafted her away with his fingertips.

'What? You don't want me to see what the food looks like?'

'It's the only way. I'll bring the pan over and feed you tiny spoonfuls so you can savour it. Then tell me the first thing that comes into your head. Okay?'

'Well, this is certainly going to be a first, but all right. I can tell you what my impressions are.'

'Excellent. But first you need to focus. All your concentration has to be on the dish. Don't mind me as I potter around. Just speak your mind. Ready?'

Sienna watched as Brett drew a tiny saucepan from the heat and left it to cool slightly on one side. She could sense her heart racing as he stepped in front of her. So close that his T-shirt was touching her dressing gown. He smelt of so many savoury odours she could almost have told him the ingredients he had been working with right there and then.

But where would the fun be in that? And, more importantly, what had he left out from the final recipe?

Her breathing sped up to match her heart as Brett hunkered down a little and flashed her one of his special killer grins as his hands moved either side of her head.

'Ready to be blown away?'

'Promises, promises. Let's go. Some of us need our beauty sleep!'

'I do wish you wouldn't talk about me like that! But you're right. Busy day tomorrow. Here we go.'

The bandana slid over her brow and rested on her nose. The last thing she saw was the burn marks on the underside of his arm as he slid the cloth lower. Her heart went out to him. He truly had suffered to get where he was.

The roof faded into a very dim glow, with only the electric lights as spots she could recognise.

'That works. Can't see a thing.'

'Excellent. I could be cooking topless and you wouldn't know.'

Oh, you are so wrong about that, she thought.

Through the faint sound of the radio in the background she could hear him rubbing the work-rough palms of his hands together as he dried them on the towel tucked into the waistband of his apron. Her whole body seemed to tune out the background noise from the electrical equipment, the hum of the refrigerator and extractor fans, and the gentle patter of the rain as it fell against the glass of the kitchen window.

And the sound of her breath as she waited for Brett to serve her something totally, totally delectable and delicious.

I want this to be the most delicious thing this amazing woman has ever tasted. Anywhere. And it's the worst mushroom sauce I have ever made in my life. What is wrong with me? I have made this in frantic, mad and busy kitchens in Hong Kong, New York and Adelaide and it was fantastic. Then I come to Rossi's and something is completely off.

He turned around just as Sienna shifted her position on what had to be the most uncomfortable chair in the city.

Then I drag this woman out of her bed in the middle of the night. In her pyjamas.

He stepped to one side and took in the view, confident that he was unlikely to be swiped around the head with something solid since she was wearing his bandana over her eyes.

Pink check pyjama bottoms which ended just below her knees. Maria's. Had to be Maria's. That probably meant that she was wearing the matching jacket under Maria's housecoat, which had certainly seen better days.

And probably nothing underneath. The only thing that separated Sienna Rossi from Brett and the outside world were two thin layers of flannelette and a wicked smile.

The metal soup ladle in Brett's hand developed a mind of its own and clattered onto the hard floor, making her jump.

'Sorry. Be with you in a moment. The temperature has to be perfect. Get ready. Three. Two. One'

He leant against the worktop, dipped a new spoon into a small bowl of the best sauce and wiped it on the edge of the saucer before lifting it carefully the few inches towards Sienna and wafting it gently in front of her nose.

Her full, luscious lips opened a little as she inhaled the aroma, and Brett carefully fed her a small spoonful of the sauce between her lips, touching the upper lip so that her tongue came out and licked the thick creamy sauce away.

It was the most erotic thing he had seen in a very, very long time.

Until now he had been totally mesmerised by her eyes. Not now. Not any longer. Her mouth was so enticing it should probably be licensed, or covered up during the daytime to prevent exposure to the unprepared.

She had the power to hold him spellbound, and the warm bowl of sauce was cooling in his hands as he stared, transfixed, at Sienna. Strange how he could not force himself to look away from that amazing mouth.

Her tongue flicked out and wiped across her lower lip, leaving a moist and succulent impression like dew on a ripe peach.

Intoxicating.

'I'm getting white wine, celery, finely chopped shallots, a touch of garlic and a sweet herb. Tarragon, and I think lemon thyme and parsley with a touch of garlic. Am I right?'

'Uh-huh. Now the mushrooms. Tell me about the mushrooms.'

He speared a few choice segments and raised them towards Sienna, whose lips were slightly apart, displaying perfect teeth, just waiting for the next delicious treat.

He paused for a second and swallowed down too many months of celibacy and many years of loneliness, then brought the spoon close enough for her to savour the aroma with a pleasing *mmm* of pleasure before he popped the mushrooms between her lips.

She chewed slowly, as though savouring every possible experience.

'This is amazing. I'm getting at least three different textures. There is a meaty earthiness in one of the mushrooms—I think it has to be dried porcini or a wild mushroom—but then I find a smooth taste which is so silky with that creamy sauce. The last one is a chestnut. I'd recognise that texture anywhere, but I have never tasted anything like this combination. It's brilliant.'

'One more,' he whispered. 'There is one extra ingredient that's going to make all the difference.'

'More? There's more? I don't know how you're going to top those mushrooms.'

Brett dipped his spoon into the second pan and tasted a mouthful of the strips of caramelised sweet onions and fresh field mushrooms with aged balsamic vinegar he was planning to use as a garnish for the chicken dish.

It was sweet, yet intensely savoury and special. And the perfect temperature.

'This is the final touch. Ready?'

She nodded once and her lips parted.

Brett wet his lips on the spoon.

Leant in. And kissed her.

She kissed him back. Sweet. Soft. Warm. Melting. Tender. Everything he had been expecting, wanting, desiring for so very long since *she* had kissed *him*.

Her hands came up and slid the blindfold away, so that her eyes were totally fixed on his. Unblinking, intense, her mouth still partly open.

'Balsamic vinegar reduction,' she whispered, her mouth only an inch from his as he held his stance with his arms stretched out on the table. 'You're right. It's the perfect final touch. And so much better than from a spoon. Can I have some more?'

This time she was the one who leant forward, so that he could kiss her more deeply, prolonging the contact between them. They broke off forehead to forehead, her breathing keeping pace with his racing heart rate as he rolled his forehead to the other side so that he could slide his unshaven chin up against her temple and back down to her mouth, the friction acting like wood to the fire.

Her eyes stayed closed as he kissed her again,

one hand pressed against the back of her head, drawing her deeper into his kiss. Deeper, and with an intensity that left them both ragged and out of breath when they broke off long enough for Sienna to lift from the chair and slide around the table, so that she could hold Brett's face and then work her sensitive fingers through his hair.

It was driving him mad.

His kisses moved over her chin, down her neck, then across to the other side, and as she tilted her head back with a sigh, she whispered, 'Promise me something?'

'Anything,' he managed to get out, before his mouth got busy on the sensitive skin on her temple.

'You will never make that exact recipe for anyone else.'

'I made it just for you. It's always been just for you.'

'In that case…what were you planning to serve for dessert?'

'Dessert? You want dessert?'

Brett froze in astonishment for a few seconds, before dropping back his head and laughing out loud with warm, joyous laughter that came from deep in his body. Wild, fun, natural and totally happy laughter that was so infectious Sienna could not resist laughing back in return, with a gentle thump on his chest.

'What's so funny?'

'You are.' He wiped away a tear of laughter with the back of a knuckle before shaking his head and lifting away a stray strand of her bed hair.

'Have you always been so demanding of your chefs, Miss Rossi?'

'Oh, this is nothing,' she replied in a mock serious voice. 'I can be much bossier when the occasion demands. Although it will be quite a challenge for you to come up with something to beat that sauce.'

She tilted her head and smiled into his face.

'I am thinking chocolate. Coffee. Cream, of course. The rest I shall leave to you.'

'Well, thank you. I'm sure I can think of something which will hit the spot!' His eyebrows lifted in a cheeky grin and she tutted in response.

'Please. I presume you are planning to serve desserts in this fabulous new restaurant of yours?'

He nodded in agreement and moved back a little. 'Speaking of which, I told you the other evening that I never break a promise—especially to a pretty lady… Well I have to break one tomorrow. But it is entirely your fault…'

'My fault?' she protested innocently. 'How can this possibly be?'

'I need to see Chris and the architects about some final decisions on the layout. That means heading across to my new kitchen. And I promised that I was all yours for a few days. On the other hand you could always come with me and cast your trained eye over my new building. Are you busy tomorrow morning?'

She closed her eyes and turned her head, so that his stubbly chin would have better access to her throat, trying to remember what day of the week it was and other unimportant things, like her name and what precisely she was doing here.

She had always known deep in her heart that Brett would be an amazing kisser, but nothing had prepared her for the depth of sensation his mouth on her throat would generate.

'Do you mean today tomorrow, or tomorrow tomorrow?'

'Today tomorrow. I'd love to show you where Chris has been spending his time these last few months.'

He moved forward to face her, his hands moving through her long loose hair and lifting it from her shoulders as it fell through his fingers—then he smoothed it down her forehead.

'You want me to visit your new restaurant?'

'Think of it as a special outing after the amazing job you did yesterday.'

He moved forward with feather-light kisses on her forehead, and she closed her eyes as his lips slid gently down to her temple, heating up the blood which was already pumping hot and fast through her body.

'*We* did a good job, Chef Cameron. Are you looking for an interior designer?

'No. But I can always use an expert opinion.'

'You make it very hard for a girl to say no.'

'Then don't. I'll make it easy. Just repeat after me— Yes, Brett, I'd like to see the kitchen where your dream will come true.'

'Well, when you put it like that… Yes, Brett, I'd *love* to see the kitchen where your dream will come true.'

'Then we have a date in about—' and he glanced over her shoulder at his wristwatch, since his hand was still busy stroking her hair '—seven hours from now. Do you think you can be ready to face the outside world by then, sleepy-head? Because I do have one suggestion—you might want to rethink your footwear before we hit the building site.'

She reluctantly forced her eyes to leave Brett's

long enough to glance at her feet. Then blinked and stared hard. Her left foot was inside a brown loafer. Only the toes of her right foot were poking daintily out from an open toed bright yellow sandal decorated with huge white daisies—Maria's summer specials.

'Oh. You see—this is what happens when I am woken up in the middle of the night by chefs looking for a food-taster.'

'In that case I shall have to do this more often.'

Sienna looked up into those hot bright eyes. There was no doubt whatsoever that he was referring to a lot more than comparing the flavour of sauce recipes.

Electrical energy crackled in the air between them—hot enough to burn paper—and her resolve crisped into white ash in the intense heat of his gaze.

She should be angry with Brett for showing her just how very wrong she had been—about so many things. But as his fingertips stroked her forehead and his lips found pleasure in the place between her jaw and throat it was impossible.

Brett Cameron had shown her that she was a woman a man like Brett could, would, *was able to* find desirable. He had even told her that she was beautiful! Every one of his touches gave her a glimpse of hope that another man *could* come to care about her.

She sucked in a breath as he found a particularly sensitive spot in the hollow behind her ear, and was rewarded with a low sigh.

Was it possible that she could fall in love again? And be loved in return?

Or was she in danger of making precisely the same mistake she had made before?

Chef-magnet.

This was all happening too fast. Too hot. And way, way, too intense for her poor brain to process what had just happened and make sense of it all.

'This has been a long day, Brett. Like I said, a girl needs her beauty sleep. And, no, that wasn't a cue for compliments.'

'You're going?'

She glanced across at the saucepans before smiling up at him. 'Maria made the right choice when she asked you to help with the cooking. I can't wait for that dessert. See you at breakfast.'

His hands moved over her shoulders and down her upper arms before he stepped back.

'Sleep well. Unless, of course, you want me to pop in and wake you up in the morning?'

She swallowed down hard at that prospect!

'Thank you, but I have my alarm clock. Goodnight, Brett. Goodnight.'

CHAPTER SEVENTEEN

Step 17: Mix with Three Heaped Spoonfuls of Tears

'I CAN hear your brain ticking from here! What's the hot topic today? Shoes? Dresses? Or let me guess. Which wine are you going to recommend for the chicken in mushroom sauce?'

Sienna half turned in the passenger seat of the Jaguar and stared at Brett in disbelief.

'I knew that you could multi-task. Nothing about mind-reading! How did you work that one out?'

He flashed a quick smile, which made Sienna grateful that she was already sitting down. 'You couldn't wait to scribble down my crazy ideas for the Valentine's Day menu this morning. Perhaps it was a mistake to talk about my seven-hour braised lamb at breakfast time?'

A puff of dismissal came from the passenger

seat. 'I think you selected those dishes just to test me. I mean, ravioli with spinach *and* blue cheese after garlic mushrooms?'

'I prefer to think of it as a challenge to a somme-lier of your talents. Guinea fowl with polenta? That has to be straightforward.'

'It would be—if you took out the parmesan and onion crisp garnish. And I really think you ought to reconsider the flavouring on the gnocchi. I'm just not sure the local high school boys are ready for that mushroom sauce.'

'Ah, but it's not for the boys, is it? That sauce is definitely one for the laydees!'

She slapped his knee with a light touch of her notebook.

'A medium red. Black cherry and plum, with some time in oak to offset the earthy mushroom flavours, but not too dry.'

'I can inhale it from here. Fantastic. What about a white?'

'Still thinking about that one,' she hissed. 'Pest.' She tapped the end of her pen against her chin. This pen was in a boring plain colour, and Brett was already missing the pink rubber flamingo.

'You must do this all the time as Head Waiter? Matching food and wine? That's quite a skill.'

'One of my favourite parts of the job. André and I can chat for hours comparing several bottles of the same grape variety from different parts of the world. I love it.'

'I can hear that in your voice. Greystone is lucky to have you. In fact, that gives me an idea. Chris has been interviewing for a sommelier for weeks. I'm going to be working flat out. Is there any chance you could sit in on the interviews and help him get though the shortlist? I need someone I can work with, who knows what they are doing! Unless of course…' He paused for a moment to focus on the road ahead, where there were multiple lanes of traffic.

'Unless?' she asked, when they were safely on a straight road.

'Unless I can steal you away from Angelo Peruzi!' he replied in a jaunty voice, completely unaware of how that simple statement ripped her apart. 'Come to work with me as my restaurant manager. Take a risk for once. Surprise yourself.'

Too late for that! She had spent most of the night after leaving the hot, hot kitchen dreaming about the life she could have with Brett by her side as her lover, if not her business partner. Working through the options. Trying to decide if she could trust this remarkable man to be her friend.

'You really don't know when to give up, do you?' Sienna replied, trying to keep her voice casual and jokey. 'I am deeply flattered, Brett. I truly am. But I know what it is like to open a new restaurant. That sort of pressure can destroy a friendship. I don't want that to happen.'

He quickly squeezed her leg in reply. 'Can't blame me for trying. I agree. Good friends are hard to come by.'

Suddenly distracted by a car horn, Brett turned back to his driving, and Sienna took a breath and looked out across the bustling London traffic to the lovely shops and art galleries they were shuffling past.

They were almost there. The narrow lanes around Notting Hill were just a few streets away.

Sienna shivered inside her coat. There was one thing that she had not told Brett when they set out that morning.

This was the first time she had been back to Notting Hill in four years. Former friends and old colleagues who lived in the area had invited her to their homes many times and she had always refused. The pain and the loss had still been too fresh.

Each street they were driving down linked her back to powerful and emotional memories which only seemed to intensify as they came closer to the site of Angelo's restaurant.

Protective instincts raised their ugly heads, poking fun at her apparent self-control, and the old anxieties rose inside her, low enough for her to master, but nagging away loud enough for her to be aware of them.

Heart racing, she turned for reassurance and support to the only person she knew would understand. Brett's face was full of all of the excitement and happy anticipation of a child on Christmas morning. It was all there for the world to see.

He started to hum along to an old song on the radio, and her heart listened and slowed a little. Tears pricked Sienna's eyes, threatening, but she blinked them away with logic.

It was only natural that she should feel a little sentimental, coming back to these streets that she'd used to know so well.

But one thing was certain: she was not going to allow her foolish anxiety to spoil Brett's day. This new restaurant was *his* dream, and he had asked her to share with him the special moment when he explored what was going to become his very own kitchen.

He had worked so hard to be driving here today. He deserved this.

Suddenly Sienna found herself joining in with Brett, happy to drink in the enthusiasm and positive energy that emanated from this finger-tapping, song-humming *tour de force*.

Without Brett she would probably never have found the strength to come back here. And with Brett? With Brett by her side she could do anything!

No tears. No trauma. Angelo's was part of her past, not her future!

She grabbed hold of that excuse for putting aside her own lingering doubts about her future role and grinned across at Brett. Friend or lover. She could still share this moment with him.

'Did you know that our restaurant used to be in Notting Hill? You've chosen a great location! And, from what Chris told me, the building work is almost complete. You must be very excited. Tell me about your plans.'

'It's a *fantastic* location! I had mixed feelings about coming back to London, but now the plans are coming together it is starting to feel as though I was meant to be here.'

He turned into a street lined by market shops and gestured from side to side. 'In fact, standing in the kitchen last night, I was thinking about my very first day at Trattoria Rossi.'

Brett laughed and slapped his hands down on the steering wheel as Sienna stared at his face, which had been transformed by such an expression of joy and pleasure it seemed as though every crease in that hard-working face was smiling.

'Maria set me to work paring and chopping vegetables for hours.' He shot her a glance. 'I'll never forget it. I was so nervous about getting it wrong I think I dropped my peeler on the floor a dozen times. I ended up spending more time washing up than actually cooking.'

They both laughed out loud, the sound of their shared laughter echoing around the confined space, warming her more than the bright sunshine.

'After a few days I progressed to actually frying onions and shallots and garlic, and by the end of my first week I was making minestrone soup.'

'Minestrone! You must have been doing something right!'

'I had a great time. Your aunt Maria gave me a chance, Sienna. Without her I would have spent a lot longer getting started in this crazy world.'

'But you would have got here in the end. Wouldn't you?'

He bowed slightly. 'Maybe, but I know that she made the difference. And of course without Maria I would never have met you!'

Sienna's heart was thumping so loudly she was sure Brett must be able to feel the vibration through the driver's seat. 'Would that have been a loss or a bonus?'

A wry smile creased one corner of his mouth, but he kept his gaze firmly on the road ahead. 'Loss. No doubt. Especially since my satellite navigation system has failed and we are now lost. Do your skills extend to navigating around Notting Hill?'

'I travelled down this road every day for eighteen months,' she replied with a dismissive snort. 'What's the address?'

Brett recited the house number and street that he had dreamt about, researched on the Internet, and planned and schemed about so often that it had become ingrained into his brain. New destination. New start. His dream come true.

'Take the next right turn,' she replied, in a faint voice tinged with anxiety. A few minutes later he pulled into the car park of the building site which was destined to be his new home, screeched to a halt and cut the engine.

He turned to look at Sienna and tried to rub some life back into her cold fingers. Winter sunshine, bright and clear, pierced the clouds and highlighted the pain in her tight-lipped face.

'What is it? Tell me what's going on.'

She seemed to come out of her trance for a moment and looked down at his hands, tracing her fingers along the scars she had never commented on before. White, pink, old and new. The scars of a working chef who had served his time.

'Look at all these cuts. Burn marks.' She lifted her head and faced him on. 'Some of us have our scars on the inside.'

He steadied himself for the hard news that was coming next. She forced herself to smile. That simple twist of her mouth and glistening eyes melted his heart.

'Please ignore me. My own restaurant was down this road. I had no idea that it would be so hard to come back. Too many memories. That's all.'

She shuffled out of her seat to stand next to him, sniffing gently, and stared past him towards the building which, to Brett's eyes, was a lot more like a restaurant than it had been a few days earlier.

'I'm okay. Really. I'm fine now.' She seemed

to give herself a mental shake, looped her arm through his and grinned. 'I want to see everything.'

A short, plump, pink-faced, dark-haired man in a warm jacket and yellow safety helmet was striding up to Sienna, and before Brett could intervene Chris thumped Brett hard on the shoulder and nodded towards Sienna with a huge grin.

'Well, I thought you would change her mind eventually. Welcome to the team, Sienna!' He stretched out his hand towards her.

She simply smiled and shook her head. 'Hello, Chris. What team? Have I missed something?'

'Our new restaurant manager, of course. I knew my boy Brett here would use his charm to win you around in the end. You have to admit his interview technique gets results with the ladies!'

Sienna stared at Chris's hand as if it was toxic waste for a second before turning to stare at Brett, who was groaning and glaring at Chris at the same time.

'Interviewing? So *that* is what you have been doing these last few days. Charming me to come and work with you. Have I understood that correctly?'

'Sienna, please.' Brett stepped in front of her, his face anxious. 'Of course I would love it if you could come and work with us, but I know you already have a great promotion. You don't understand…'

'Oh, on the contrary. I understand very well indeed. Nice meeting you again, Mr Fraser. Good luck finding someone willing to work with this idiot! In the meantime, I'll take the bus back.'

And with that she turned and walked away from them, back towards the road, one hand pressed firmly against her mouth, preventing them from seeing her bitter tears.

Only she never reached it. With a slight stagger, she leant against the wall for support, her legs unsteady and threatening to give way beneath her.

Brett stood there, frozen, watching Sienna retreat inside herself to a place where he could not go. He barely recognised the woman who had leapt into his car with a spring in her step that morning.

Ignoring the fact that Chris and other members of his design team were coming up to greet him, Brett wound his way around the front of his car, looped his arm around Sienna's waist and half carried her as far as the passenger door, where she had some hope of catching her breath, or at least passing out with some dignity.

She faltered on the icy path, and as he held her

tighter around the waist, taking her weight, he felt her heart beating under her sweater in the cold air. He knew his fate was sealed as he lowered her into the passenger seat.

She looked up at him in surprise, and then, as though recognising something in him she could trust until her dying day, she stared, white faced, into his concerned eyes.

'Do not say a word. Not one word. Simply get me out of here, Brett.'

'You got it.'

Brett grabbed his padded jacket and wrapped it around her shoulders, but he knew it would take more than a coat to stop this precious woman from shivering.

Doomed.

He was completely in love with Sienna Rossi.

No going back. This was it. He was going to find out who and what had broken this remarkable woman's heart and not stop until he had put those fractured pieces back together again.

Sienna squirmed against the sofa cushions and half opened her eyes, blinking in the glare from a single table light. She was leaning on something soft and pale blue.

She had fallen sideways, and her head was pressed into Brett's shoulder.

Horrified, she slid back to a sitting position and squeezed her eyes shut again as she yawned widely with both hands over her mouth.

When she opened them, Brett was scratching his scalp. It was a gesture she had seen him perform dozens of times before. Right hand, right side of his head, just above the ear. It was a wonder he was not bald in that spot.

'Looking for inspiration?'

He went pink around the neck, but stayed focused on the clever photos of perfect dishes on the pages of a book with a photo of a TV chef on the cover.

'I was hoping that this pastime would make me look more intellectual. On second thoughts, don't answer that. Not many girls fall asleep on me. This could be a bad sign.'

Sienna rubbed the back of her neck, turning her head from side to side.

'Sorry about using you for a pillow. Most embarrassing. Of course I blame you completely, for forcing me to drink hot chocolate on an empty stomach. Always knocks me sideways. How long was I out?'

'Over two hours. And you're welcome to cuddle up to me any time you like.'

He broke the tension then, by raising his eyebrows up and down a few times.

'Oh, slick. Very slick,' Sienna said, and grinned at him as she slid her feet to the carpet and stretched forward to take both of Brett's hands as he helped her stand.

He smiled back before replying in a soft voice, 'That's better. You always did have the cutest smile, Rossi. Even if you *are* dressed as a polar explorer.'

She stuck out the arms of her thick sweater and plucked at the cuffs. 'I work in air-conditioned restaurants and stone buildings all year round, but when I see real weather outside. Brrrr…'

She lifted away one corner of Maria's living-room curtains to demonstrate her point. And stared out. Open mouthed.

'It's snowing,' she eventually managed to pronounce, in a low, intense whisper.

Sienna almost pressed her nose to the glass, ignoring the vibration and engine noise of the cars whizzing past on the busy road on the other side of the pavement.

It *was* snowing. It was truly snowing. She could actually see the flakes against the darkness of the evening sky as they reflected back the light from the headlamps of passing cars and streetlights.

It was one of the most magical things she had ever seen.

'Brett! Look!' Without hesitation or thinking she grabbed his hand and hugged him tight against her so that he could see out of the window.

A wide grin spread out across his face, and she laughed out loud as he grabbed her by the waist and pulled her closer, so that the white flakes appeared to come straight at them through the layers of glass.

At that moment a large truck trundled past, momentarily blocking out the light, and the glass surface was instantly transformed into a mirror. Sienna found herself looking at two happy faces reflected in the glass.

Cameron and Rossi. Best team she had ever worked in.

Her head was pressed into Brett's neck, and he pressed his body along one side of hers so that he could share the first sight of snowflakes.

He was grinning, open-mouthed. So was she.

They were two happy people.

Then his smile faded—as did hers.

The reflection in the mirror window changed as Brett turned a few inches, so that she was close enough to feel his fast breath on her cheeks. She had nowhere to look but into his eyes.

His deep, intense, smiling eyes.

Laser probes burrowed into her skull and turned the sensible girl into mush.

His hand was still at her waist. The other meshed his fingers between hers and squeezed tightly as he spoke, his eyes never leaving hers.

'It's lovely.' *You are lovely*. 'Chris made a mistake this afternoon. I respect your choices.'

'I know. Going back to that street was just all too much for me. I feel quite foolish.'

He took a breath and his eyes scanned her face, as though checking that she was real. It was a millisecond before her neck was burning and her breathing had speeded up to match his.

'Not foolish at all,' he said, and smiled at her. 'But I do think it is time you told me exactly why you can't trust chefs. Stay right there!'

Suddenly he released her and slipped out of the room, leaving her staring ahead at the space he had occupied, while her heart rate struggled to return to normal. And failed.

Something inside her clicked into gear.

He deserved the truth. Even if it meant going back to a place she thought she had left behind.

CHAPTER EIGHTEEN

Step 18: And Two Pink Cupcakes

BRETT BREEZED back into the room, carrying a tray with two steaming beakers and a paper bag with pink glittery stars glued on it, which he opened and presented to her. He collapsed down on the sofa, completely unfazed by the fact that she was still standing at the window, staring out at the snowflakes with childlike fascination.

'Chris came round when you were having your nap. He says sorry for the misunderstanding about the job, and a big hi and thank you from Jess. You are now officially one of the princess gang, and I am commanded to present Your Royal Highness with these fine examples of baked goods as a token of their esteem. Apparently the nanny made them from a packet mix.'

He held up two pink cupcakes, each with a

single pink cake candle sticking out from the centre, held in place by a thick blob of white icing.

Sienna and Brett both stared at the candles for a second in silence.

'Jess does have style. Decaf?'

All Sienna could manage was a single nod, and it took her several delicious sips of the hot, bitter-sweet drink before she was ready to speak.

'Brett?'

'Mmm?' he replied, between mouthfuls.

'Sorry about being so upset earlier. I'm…embarrassed about—well, what I must have looked like, and how my reaction was completely over the top. I had no right to be annoyed with you. Sorry.'

He shook his head and pursed his lips. 'You're not the one who should feel sorry. I should have made it clear to Chris that you had to make your own mind up and that I'd respect your decision either way. My mistake.'

He brushed crumbs into the paper bag, before sliding to the edge of the sofa. 'Now, I am under strict instructions that you have to eat one whole cupcake, or you are not an official princess.'

Sienna looked at the cake and swallowed hard. 'I don't think I can.'

'One whole cake. I promised Jess. And nobody goes hungry in this house.'

He slid the tray closer towards her.

'Slave driver,' she replied, but, since he was staring at her so intently, started peeling off the paper and broke the cake into two.

'That's better,' he said, reaching for his second.

'Hey!'

He brushed more crumbs from his fingers onto the tray. 'Okay. I'm ready to hear the whole story. We have coffee. We have something close to cake. Start talking. You can skip the bit about how his Hollywood charm made you swoon and get straight to the bit where you were working together at Angelo's restaurant. What really happened? What went wrong? And why did Frank not break his nose for you? Because I cannot believe for one minute that Angelo Peruzi dumped you. He's not *that* much of an idiot.'

'Yes, he is.' She found something very fascinating in the paper case. 'It's quite simple, really. Angelo Peruzi fell out of love with me, ran our business into the ground, and ran back home to California. He broke my heart and walked out on me. But in the end I was the one who broke up with him.' She paused.

'About a month before our wedding, I started taking calls from suppliers asking when their bills were going to be paid. Angelo insisted on taking care of all of the financial side of the restaurant, so I mentioned it to him straight away. He said it must be a mistake at the bank and he would sort it out and not to bother him again.' She lowered her head and shrugged. 'He hated to be challenged. About anything. Angelo had worked with his father in their restaurant all his life, and his food was amazing. He had the looks and the talent, and as far as he and his family were concerned he was the golden boy who could do no wrong.'

She smiled apologetically. 'I was not the only one who was dazzled by him. My family adored him. Until…the cracks started to appear. It was hard for him to admit that he couldn't handle the business side of things *and* run the kitchen and do promotional work and the thousand and one things he wanted to achieve. All at once.'

Brett rubbed the back of Sienna's neck—her strain was only too apparent.

'I was organising the wedding. He was in denial and refused to admit that he couldn't cope. Call it pride, arrogance—whatever. The end result was the same. We had a brilliant kitchen brigade and full tables every night. I had no idea that there was a problem with finance.'

Tiny fragments of cupcake icing had found their way onto her jumper, and she slowly picked them off, one by one, as Brett held her in silence.

'I remember the day I had to say goodbye to the staff—the tears, the hugs, the hours I spent sobbing alone that night after I'd closed the door for the last time.'

'Alone? You mean, he didn't even come back to thank his team? He left you here to handle the mess on your own?'

'He claimed that it would be too expensive to fly back for a few days, but I knew it was going to be too painful for him. Too traumatic.'

She shook her head from side to side. 'I still trusted him and believed in him. Even then. Angelo kept telling me that once the London restaurant was sold he would be able to pay off all of his debts and I would be free to move to Los Angeles and make our new home together in California.'

The muscles in Brett's neck clenched at the tension in her voice, and the anger rose in his soul as he suspected what was coming next.

'You know what really hurt?' she continued in

a low voice. 'It wasn't the money, or that we had to sell the business. That was nothing compared to the fact that Angelo did not *tell* me there was a problem. I would have understood in a heartbeat. We were supposed to be partners! He knew that I would do anything for him—and that I trusted him without question.'

'He didn't know you,' Brett whispered.

'You're right. And I didn't know him, either. Perhaps that why it was such a surprise when he packed his bags and told me that he needed to go home for a few weeks. On his own. I thought *I* was his home.'

She gave a sarcastic laugh, but the tears still pricked her eyes as Brett asked her the question which had puzzled him from the start.

'I'm still confused about one thing. Why did you tell people that he had dumped you and headed back home? The truth was bound to come out eventually.'

'I didn't tell people anything. The family knew why I had broken off my engagement, but everyone else came to their own conclusions when Angelo did not come back. As for the truth? The Rossi family closed ranks and came to the conclusion that being duped once was humiliating enough for me, but being duped twice? That would make me a laughing stock. So no. The truth never came out. The suppliers were paid. And he got away with it. What a lucky escape. Eh?'

She had wrapped her arms around her body, as though trying to warm herself and block out the bone-penetrating icy wind and the snowflakes on the other side of the window glass.

Brett waited for her to go on, but her voice had grown gradually quieter and more choked as she spoke. Her last words were so full of pain that he felt a shiver of cold run across her shoulders and down her back.

He zipped open his own padded fleece jacket and stepped behind her, pressing his shirtfront against her back, his arms circling her waist, so that she was totally enclosed inside his warm embrace.

Neither of them spoke for a few minutes as Brett followed her gaze out to the snowflakes, his head pressed against her shoulder.

Her head fell forward. 'I should have known. It took him a total of three days after we sold the business to build up the courage to make the telephone call telling me that he thought we should take a break before I flew out to join him. It took me all of ten seconds to realise that he didn't want me. I had ceased to be useful. He was far too cowardly to admit that he did not love me any more, so I did the only thing I could do. I told him it was over. Not the best way for a relationship to end.'

'What did you do?'

A snort and a chuckle. 'I packed up the few possessions I had left and went home to my old bedroom in the Rossi house. I was exhausted, lonely, vulnerable, more than a little depressed, and very, very angry. At everyone! The family persuaded me not to get on a plane to California and confront him face to face, and it was my aunt Maria who gave me sanctuary until I was ready to start work again. I owe her just as much as you do—so thank you for helping me find a way to repay her.'

She glanced up at him over her right shoulder, and the pain in those limpid brown eyes was only too apparent through the faint smile.

Brett looked deep into those eyes and his heart melted.

After all she had been through, she still had the capacity for happiness.

She was remarkable!

He closed his eyes. He was holding Sienna Rossi in his arms, and it felt so right. So very right. How had he doubted that this was what he wanted? What he needed?

There was no way he could allow her to walk away from him.

Slowly, slowly, he dropped his hands to her waist and started to turn her around to face him.

As though awakening from a dream, Sienna realised that she was not alone, and her head twisted towards him inside the huge jacket. As her body turned slowly his hands shifted, so that when her chin was pressed against the front of his shirt his arms were around her back, pressing her forward.

In silence, his eyes closed, and he listened to her breathing, her head buried into the corner of his neck and throat.

Her arms, which had been trapped inside his fleece, moved to circle around his waist, so that she could hold him closer.

A faint smile cracked Brett's face. She was hugging him back. Taking his warmth and devotion.

He dared not risk taking it any further. Dared not break that taste of trust she was offering him.

But Brett edged closer, hugging her tighter, and dropped his face a little so that his lips were in the vicinity of her forehead.

Sienna responded immediately, and looked up

as he moved back just far enough so that their eyes locked.

For that single moment everything that had gone before meant nothing. They were a man and a woman who cared for one another very deeply, holding each other.

It seemed the most natural thing in the world for Brett to run his lips across her upturned forehead, then her closed eyes. He felt her mouth move against his neck. Stunned with the shock of the sensation, he almost jerked away, but then paused and pressed his face closer to hers, his arms tight on her back, willing his love to pass through his open hands, through the clothing to her core of her body.

Warming her. Begging her to trust him. But not daring to say the words that might break the spell.

This was unreal.

A single beam of light streamed out from a passing car on the road and caught on Sienna's face, like a spotlight. The golden light warmed her skin. They were both cold, but there was no way Brett would break this precious moment when the barriers were down and he could express what words would fail to convey.

His hands slid up and down her back. His mouth

moved across her cheek and he felt her lift her chin. Waiting for his kiss.

Adrenaline surged through his body, all his senses alive to the stunning woman he was holding in his arms. His heart was racing, and he could feel her breath warm as they looked into each other's eyes, both of them open-mouthed. Nose almost touching nose. His head tilted. Ready.

For the kiss that never came.

It was Sienna who stepped away, sliding out of his arms.

'I felt so worthless. When Angelo left, he took every bit of confidence and self-esteem I ever had with him. It's taken me four years to piece together what was left of my shattered life, one day at a time, and rebuild a future for myself. I promised myself that I was never going to rely on someone else to make my dreams come true ever again. And I've kept that promise. I *have* to make my own way in the world. You understand what that is like better than anyone I have ever met. Don't you?'

He tucked her hair behind her ear and gently smoothed the strands away from her brow before replying in a slow whisper. Intimate and soft, and so loving it hurt to hear it.

'Yes. I do. Which leaves one final question. You

may not *need* a man in your life, but is there any room in this plan for a man who cares about you and wants to be with you?'

She swallowed down a breath of understanding and replied with a quivering lower lip. She had seen through him yet again.

'I don't know, Brett. I truly don't know. This job at Greystone has been my only goal for so long I never thought about what came next.'

There was so much confusion and anxiety in her face that Brett took the initiative. He would have to work through the next steps more slowly than he wanted if he had any chance of convincing Sienna to make him part of her life. Biting down frustration and disappointment, he managed a smile before rubbing her arms for one last time this evening.

'I don't know about you, but this has been a very long day and we have the excitement of re-stocking the kitchen cabinets tomorrow. Come prepared to be grilled about this amazing new job of yours. How does that sound?'

A faint smile creased her pale and exhausted-looking face, but she slowly stepped away.

'Well, that *is* something to look forward to. Goodnight, Brett. Sleep well.'

'Goodnight, sweetheart.'

She faltered slightly, stopped in the doorway, and glanced back at him over one shoulder.

Her glance only lasted a few seconds, but something unravelled inside him.

It was as though a door which had been locked tight shut for too many years had been opened up. Rusty. Hesitant. Resisting. A large, heavy door, with a huge lock and chain across it, and a sign saying: 'Worthless. Unworthy of the love of an amazing woman.' Only now the chain had been lifted away and the door had swung open.

This was the same locked door that had made it impossible for him to tell Lili that he loved her. The lock had turned tighter each time he saw how happy she'd been with Chris. The extra chain had come the day his mother had died of a stroke, walking home from her night office cleaning job only a few months before he won his promotion to head chef. She had never had the chance to stand next to him at an awards ceremony, or see his name in the newspapers. He had wanted that more than anything else in his life.

He had created that lock and chain to protect his sensitive and tender emotions from the searing, traumatic pain of loss. To keep them safe and carefully hidden away.

As he looked at Sienna in that fraction of a second each instinct from his broken childhood should have screamed for him to turn the key in the lock and slam that door tight shut again. But instead they were blown away by the force of a hot wind so powerful that he had to physically stand taller to brace himself against the force of it.

He stood in silence, the breath catching in his throat as she tried to smile and failed. The pain in her lovely shining brown eyes shone out and hit him hard.

It was all there in her face. Her lips were parted and her cheeks flushed as if they had just spent the night together.

A warm soft feeling of tenderness and love enveloped Brett and he moved forward to hold her tight against him, but she gasped and shook her head, started to say something, thought better of it, bit her lower lip, turned in his arms and slipped away out of the room.

Leaving him standing there.

His head spinning at the turmoil going on inside his heart.

He had survived childhood by deliberately not making any connections and refusing to love anyone enough to make a difference.

The feelings he had for Sienna were terrifying, exhilarating—and challenged him more than he wanted to admit.

Only a few days earlier he had imagined that opening his new restaurant was going to be the biggest adventure of his life. Well, he had been wrong. Winning over the whirlwind that was Sienna Rossi meant more.

Telling her how much he loved her was going to be one of the biggest risks he had ever taken—he knew that she cared about him. Now all he had to do was prove that he was worth taking the risk on.

The door was open and passion and determination flooded out creating an echoing empty space where love was meant to dwell.

He had already lost Lili.

No matter how long it took or how creative he was going to have to become, he was going to be the man to show Sienna Rossi that she was loved.

He was not going to lose Sienna. Not now. Not ever.

He had to think, and think fast.

Sienna had made it clear that she did not need or want any man telling her how to run her life. Now he understood why!

Only she thought that she had a few limited options to choose from, where she could be free to make that possible. Perhaps she was mistaken about that? After all, he had seen her transform Trattoria Rossi into a perfect small local diner. Any family would be happy to eat there....

The perfect family diner...was it possible?

Flicking open his cellphone, Brett quickly found the number for his best friend.

'Chris, mate. How are you doing? Yes, I told Sienna. She was okay. Listen. Is there any chance you could come over here tonight? I would like to talk through a crazy business idea you might be interested in.'

CHAPTER NINETEEN

Step 19: Add One American Chef Without a Kilt

'HI, CARLA. Yes, I'm fine. How are things at the Manor? Yes. I'm sorry that I had to leave so suddenly. What's the best time for me to avoid…? He's what? Any idea when?'

Sienna pinched the brow of her nose tight enough to be painful. 'No. Of course I understand. Patrick is still the boss. Thank you for letting me know. I'll talk to you later.'

She flung the phone down before Carla could answer.

'That interfering—!'

Sienna pressed both hands down firmly onto the hall table to steady herself and closed her eyes to block out the nausea.

'Unbelievable!'

There was a rustle of plastic wrapping from the

sitting room, where Brett had been unpacking some of his personal saucepans, and the man himself appeared in the doorway.

She looked up at his smiling face and marvelled at his ability to calm her and reassure her in one single glance.

'Did I hear shouting? Where is the fire?'

Sienna raised one hand and waved it in Brett's direction, before pressing it to the back of her head as she started to pace up and down the hallway in the mid-morning light streaming through the glass panel over Maria's front door.

'Patrick. The general manager at Greystone. He has arranged a planning meeting for the design team for the new restaurant. Apparently Angelo is only in town for a few days, and they want to go through the first ideas before he heads back to California. They didn't even think about calling me until the very last minute! If Carla hadn't reminded Patrick he probably would have completely forgotten to invite me.'

She was gesticulating now, using both hands to strangle imaginary demons in the air, her mind buzzing with excitement and enthusiasm. 'As the new restaurant manager I *need* to be there. I have so many ideas, Brett, but this meeting has come completely out of the blue. I don't even have time to put together a formal presentation to the team!'

Her enthusiasm was infectious, and he smiled right at her before replying in a calm voice, 'This sounds like the ideal chance for you to make a difference as the new manager. When is the meeting?'

Her voice trembled with frustration. 'That's why I'm jumping.' She glanced at her wristwatch, totally absorbed in the momentum of the news. 'Carla has been told to expect them in about four hours. Four hours—*today*, Brett! I need to be there before they arrive, and then start work straight way on a detailed plan. There are so many things to get sorted out before Angelo takes over that I hardly know where to start.'

Brett took one look at her dancing eyes and knew that her mind certainly wasn't on helping him clean out the kitchen units—or any other excuse he could come up with to be in the same room as her. He had never seen her so animated.

This was how it should be. The scared woman he had soaked with a bucket of water was gone for good. Replaced with a professional manager who was at the top of her game.

The Sienna Rossi he was looking at now

sounded confident, self assured and assertive about her new role. Just as he knew she could be.

He wondered how she would react if she knew that he had spent most of the night talking about her to Chris, while they thrashed out an idea for a new business where *she* could be the star. If she wanted it! But it was far too early to tell her about that option. There were still a lot of questions which had to be answered before the deal was final.

Pity that something just did not sound right about her situation at Greystone. He had the most horrible feeling that this amazing woman was about to have her dream trampled to dust under her feet. And that was not fair.

'Are you sure that they actually *want* you to be there for this meeting, Sienna?'

She stopped pacing and looked at him with a slight frown. 'What do you mean? I'm the person who is going to have to make the new dining room work after the paint has dried! Of *course* they want me there. Patrick simply forgot that I was on holiday. That's all.'

'So Patrick and Angelo just have to snap their fingers and you come running? Is that right?'

'Brett! I thought you would be happy for me.' There was such pain and disappointment in her voice that he walked swiftly up to her and took hold of one of her hands in his, meshing his fingers between hers so that she could not escape.

She was so shocked at this that she flashed open her eyes and stared at the offending appendage as though it did not belong to her at all.

'I am happy for you. I simply think you're forgetting something very important. You are an amazing, beautiful and talented woman, and any man would be honoured to have you in his life or on his management team. I have a few concerns.'

'Go on. I'm listening. But make it fast.'

'The way I see it, you have two ways to handle this meeting.' He looked hard into her face, his voice low and serious.

Sienna was about to give her opinion about people who defined *her* choices, when Brett reached out with a not so clean forefinger and pressed it to her lips.

'First choice. Angelo Peruzi pulls up at the hotel with his fancy team of architects and designers. You graciously welcome him in, the two of you make small talk about the weather and the state of the restaurant business and then you start work on the design of your new award-winning dining room. *Together*. As a team. No past history, just focused on the job.'

He moved his hand from left to right. 'He talks, you listen politely, then accept or decline his suggestions in a ladylike dignified and professional fashion and wave at the door as he drives away.' There was a pause. 'Or maybe not so professional, depending on what he has to say. You are totally in charge of the situation and he knows it.'

Sienna started squirming again but Brett continued. 'Stop that. There are pluses to this plan. Best-case scenario: he falls at your feet, begs your forgiveness and tells you that it will be an honour and a privilege to work with you and he has total respect for you in your new role. You both go off into the sunset, or whatever, hand in hand and destined for greatness.'

'Have you been sniffing the icing sugar again?' Sienna replied with a frown.

He ignored her snipe with a brief narrowing of his eyes. 'Worst case: you have to suffer your ex for an hour or so over a conference table. But then the deed is done, the ice is broken, and you can get on with your life and start work on creating something amazing. Worst part over. You've done your duty to Patrick and the team, and maybe Peruzi has an apology for you. It could happen.'

He squeezed her hand once before releasing it. 'But you always have to have a back-up plan. So, onto your second choice… You go back to the Manor, take one look at what this team are proposing, give it up as a lost cause and look for another job somewhere else.'

Sienna gasped and slapped him on the chest.

'Have you not been listening to *anything* I have been telling you these last few days? All I am asking for is the chance to show them what I am capable of achieving. This job will give me that chance, and I am *not* taking no for an answer.'

Her brow furrowed into a deep frown of concern and anxiety.

'You don't know how hard it is has been for me to rebuild my confidence. This is what I want. It's what I've always wanted, and I've worked too long to let this chance slip away from me. I *have* to prove that I can do this work.'

'Prove it to Angelo? Or prove it to yourself?'

Brett's free hand touched her arm, thrilling her with the heat and warmth of his support. 'You're Sienna Rossi. The unconquerable! Have you not just designed, decorated and refurbished one complete dining room on your own? You can *do* this job—but you don't have to. You've already shown what you are capable of. Right here. At Rossi's. You don't need to go back to Greystone Manor and settle for what they have to offer you just because it is comfortable. There are other hotels and restaurants who would love to have you work for them.'

Sienna wriggled and pulled and tugged to free herself—then suddenly she stopped fighting him and sagged down with a resigned sigh.

'Wait a minute. Does that list include Brett Cameron of Notting Hill?'

He sucked in a breath. 'Yes. It does. The job is yours if you want it. But there are others. You have more choices than you know.'

The last few days flashed though her brain. The shared meals, the laughter and the pizza party with the kids. The jokes and glimpses of their pasts. Could she walk away from all that?

Slipping her fingers out from between his, Sienna broke away and stepped back to look at Brett, well aware of the fierce intensity in his eyes.

'You truly don't understand. I could *never* work for you.'

'You can't mean that.'

'It's not you, and I know that the job would be fantastic! I totally admire and respect what you are trying to achieve there. No, Brett. It's me.'

She cupped the palms of both of her hands against his cheeks, her fingers tingling from contact with the blond stubble, and looked deep into his eyes. Pleading for his understanding.

'This is my dream. The dream I created for myself when things were very dark in my life. That means that I am the only person who can see it through to the end. Not Angelo. Not Patrick… And not you. I can only rely on myself.'

'Maybe once. But you must know that I am here for you,' he butted in. 'You don't have to do this on your own.'

She nodded and sniffed. 'I'm sorry if that sounds hard, but it is the truth—and I always tell my close friends the truth. And I hope we *are* friends. I really do. Because people who care about me are in pretty short supply in my life.'

Brett sighed loudly, and before she could go anywhere pulled her towards him, gathered her into his arms and pressed his lips to her forehead.

'You're not coming back to Rossi's. Are you?'

Her answer was a brief shake of the head.

'So that's it? You're just going to walk out on me? On us?'

Her cheek rested flat against his shirt before she found the strength to speak, not trusting her resolve if she saw his face.

'In a few days from now you are going to be working flat out in your new kitchen. Seven days a week. Catching a few hours' sleep when you can.'

'Have you been talking to Chris?' His voice rumbled below the fabric she was leaning on.

'I've been there once before. Remember? Oh, Brett.' She moved back so that her fingers stroked his shirt in gentle circles. 'We're both going to be working harder than we have ever worked in our lives. I don't want either of us to resent the time we steal to be together. That's not fair. On anyone. These last few days have been so unexpected. Thank you for that. But, no. I won't be coming back.'

He ran his fingers through her hair one last time, kissed her gently on the forehead, and then on the lips with the sweetest kiss of her life, and finally he wrapped her tight against him until he was ready to whisper a few words.

'I can't let you go. Not like this. There's so much I haven't told you. So much I want to say—' But his words were silenced.

'Shh. It's okay. It's okay. I am going to leave now, while we still have hope. It's better this way for both of us than facing heartbreak down the line. We both know what that feels like…and I'm not sure I could come back if I had my heart broken again this time.' Her fingers stroked his face as he released his grip. 'You have to let me go. That way we can both hold onto something special. Because you are so very special. Never forget that.'

A deep shudder racked Brett's body, but she felt his heartbeat slow down just a little under her fingers.

The sensation of his hands sliding away from her back was so painful she almost cried out with the loss. He was letting her go. And she was already missing his touch.

'I'm going to miss having someone around to remind me of that. If you have to do this, do it now—before I change my mind. I'll give you a lift to the station.'

Sienna stood, rock-steady now, her back pressed hard against the door.

Brett took hold of both of her arms and looked into her eyes, his love and devotion so open and exposed it was like a whirlwind of confusion and suppressed energy.

'Sienna? You already know how stubborn I can be. This isn't the end. Whatever options you choose, I'll be right here if you need me. *You* never forget *that*.'

He watched as she took a breath, looked him straight in the eyes, gave a sharp nod and then ran up the stairs to get ready to leave, the sound of her footsteps echoing back into the hallway.

'We still have a date here on Valentine's Day—and I'm making your favourite dessert, just the way you like it.'

'You don't know my favourite dessert!' came a distant voice, before the bedroom door closed shut.

Oh, yes, he did. He knew everything he needed to know about the woman he had fallen in love with. Just when he'd thought that his poor guarded heart would never be open to love again.

Brett could feel his throat closing with emotion, and struggled to pull the shattered fragments of his willpower together.

Even the thought of not being with Sienna twisted his heart tight enough to make him gasp. Suddenly the rosy future he had been looking forward to so desperately seemed dark and grey if Sienna was not part of it.

He had two choices. Tell her that he loved her.

Or let her go in the full knowledge that the hectic lives they led would make a relationship so difficult it might destroy them with the guilt of all the missed birthdays and special occasions normal couples could hope to enjoy.

She was right about that.

But it would be worth it for every single second of time they spent together.

No. He could not be so selfish. Not with Sienna. Not with the woman he loved.

If he told her how he felt about her…how she had come to dominate his thoughts and his dreams…how he longed to see her, hold her, simply be with her…there was a chance that she might stay for the sake of their relationship—at the cost of her own ambitions at Greystone Manor.

Telling her that he loved her now would only make it worse for both of them. Once said, the words could never be unsaid. And then what? What kind of pressure would that create?

This was Sienna's dream!

He had waited ten long exhausting years to make his own dream come true.

How could he deny this amazing woman the chance to do the same?

He had to let this tender, funny, clever woman

walk away and make her own dreams a reality before he could come to her on equal terms and build something where they could both achieve their goals.

He had never thought of himself as noble, but if there was ever a time for sacrifice, this was it.

Even if it did rip his heart out.

CHAPTER TWENTY

Step 20: Beat Vigorously

SIENNA STOOD in front of the full-length mirror in the stone-walled tower room of Greystone Manor, which had been her safe refuge for the last four years, and ran both hands down over her fine cashmere knee-length skirt to smooth away any creases.

She had spent time and money choosing the perfect black skirt suit and glossy designer shoes. It was easy to make the excuse that fine-dining customers expected a certain level of formality in the waiting staff, but the truth was harder to accept.

The last few days had shown her how much she missed working with wine and flavours and colour. Creating something amazing and unique which she knew in her heart that Maria's customers would love.

This suit was part of the armour she wore every

day to convince everyone that she was totally in control and in charge as head waiter.

It was pathetic. *She* was pathetic.

Brett was right.

She was a coward. A brave woman hiding behind a façade she had made for herself.

She had needed these tall, solid walls to give her time to rebuild her confidence that she was capable and able to do her job without a controlling man telling her what to do.

When would she ever get the chance to do that again?

Sienna strolled over to her window that overlooked the stunning grounds of the hotel and let the tears fall in silence down her cheeks, ruining her make-up.

She had looked at this view for four long years, but the hotel had never felt like home. A safe place? Yes. But not home. Closing her eyes, she could still see the view from the spare bedroom in Maria's house, of the busy London street, and longed to be back there.

The vibration of her cellphone broke the spell with a simple text message from Carla.

The design team had arrived. It was time to get this over with once and for all.

* * *

Carla was hidden behind a large contingent of men in suits carrying art portfolios and packaging tubes, who were being greeted by senior hotel management from across Europe.

Sienna sucked in a breath and lifted her chin, stretching herself to her full height and fixing a professional smile firmly in place.

In the centre of the laughing, happy group gathered in the reception area of Greystone Manor was the man she had last seen at the departure gate before his flight to Los Angeles.

Angelo Peruzi.

On that fateful day she had watched in silence as he had walked through passport control and out of view. He had not looked back at her. Not once. He had not spared one backward glance at the woman he had asked to be his wife only a few months earlier.

Today Angelo Peruzi was wearing almost the same clothing he had worn that day—a navy blazer, white pressed shirt and designer denims. And dark sunglasses.

In February.

Indoors, in a country house hotel.

She had forgotten how very handsome he was. The years had filled out his face, and there was a certain softness about his body, but life in California had served Angelo well. Every inch of his designer clothing screamed success and wealth.

He looked as though one of the photographer's stylists had spent a couple of hours working on him with false tan and teeth whitener to impress TV viewers. He probably had no idea how strange and out of place they made him look in this elegant, dignified house.

Sienna locked eyes with Angelo across the room. For a fleeting second she felt as though they were the only people present.

His brow creased slightly in recognition, before he flashed her one of his special smiles and made his way through the group of men in smart suits to stand in front of her. He stretched out his hand.

'Sienna. It's so good to see you again. You look wonderful. Perhaps we can catch up next week?'

'Of course,' she managed to reply through a closed throat, and was saved by Patrick, who had never left Angelo's side.

'Ah, Miss Rossi. Thank you for coming in at such short notice. I apologise for breaking into your holiday, but we only have a tiny window for a meeting with Chef Peruzi, and I know that you want to hear our exciting plans for the new dining room! Please join us. I know that you are going to be totally thrilled with the proposal.'

Thirty minutes later two things had suddenly become very clear.

She was not thrilled with the new proposals. *At all.*

The hotel management had brought in a top team of slick restaurant designers who had taken one look at the lovely antique wooden panels on the walls and the intricate ceiling work in the original hall and tutted. Loudly. This was *not* the space they had planned for the new Peruzi restaurant.

She had twice tried to make a suggestion. And twice been dismissed and talked down. Neither Patrick nor Angelo had spoken up for her, or given her the slightest hint of support and encouragement when she had argued against the obliteration of the very architectural features which made the Manor so unique.

The design team were not interested in anything she had to say—which was hard to believe, considering the outlandish ideas they were proposing.

Californian fusion? *At Greystone?*

Patrick she could understand—his bosses had paid this team of so-called experts to create a 'unique vision' for the new restaurant. He could hardly tell them they were crazy!

The second fact was even harder to accept.

Sienna took a long, hard look at Angelo, who was looking disdainfully around the beautiful oak panelled room, and wondered how they had both come to change so very much in so short a time.

He had walked out of her town, her family and her life, and now he had just waltzed into the hotel as though he was the cavalry who was going to save them all from disaster.

As though she ought to be grateful that he had taken the time out of his busy schedule to lower himself to say hello. No apology. No explanation. Not even an excuse for what had happened to the restaurant he had abandoned, leaving her to sort out the mess he had left behind.

At least he had not tried to kiss her. Simply shaken her hand.

This was what she wanted. Wasn't it?

For Angelo to treat her as simply one of his colleagues?

She looked across at the slight sneer on Angelo's mouth and in that second the reality of the man hit her hard and fast. This was not the Angelo she remembered!

That Angelo had been some fictitious, imaginary ideal. A mirage. A version she had put together from her own imagination. She had been infatuated with an idealised clone of a man who had never truly existed.

Whatever relationship they might have had once was long gone. That part of her life was finished.

There was a very good chance that he would destroy everything André Michon had built up. And she wanted no part of it. In fact, the more she thought about it, the more she realised that it would have been a horrible mistake for her to come back and try and work with Angelo under *any* circumstances.

Brett Cameron had shown her what it could be like to work with someone she trusted and who respected her opinion. Valued her. Cared for her. Maybe more than just cared for her.

Which made her the biggest fool in the world.

A wave of nausea and dizziness hit Sienna, forcing her to lean against the table for support. The coffee. She should have eaten breakfast. Now just the thought of food made her dizzier than ever, and she fought to get air into her lungs.

Sienna tried to control her breathing, and lifted her chin just as Patrick caught her eye and waved his empty coffee cup from side to side, gesturing towards the door.

Yes. It *was* time to leave the room. Only it wouldn't be to make more coffee. It would be to start packing.

CHAPTER TWENTY-ONE

Step 21: Finish with One Portion of Chocolate Tiramisu

SIENNA BENT down from the waist onto the pristine white dining-room tablecloth with her arms flopped down each side of her body, and bobbed her head down twice onto the hard surface before resting her forehead on the cloth.

'I think Patrick got the message in the end,' Carla said as she gathered together the glassware in the now empty dining room at the end of evening service. 'Apparently he has never had anyone resign from a management job before. It's a new experience for him.'

Sienna did not even attempt to raise her head to reply, so the words that did emerge were muffled by a lot of blubbering and a tang of self-pity.

'Perhaps you shouldn't have asked him for a

reference? That might have been a bit cheeky? Anyway—stay right there. I'll be back in a moment with dessert, and you can tell me all the lovely details.'

A loud groan followed by a whimper coincided with the sound of her forehead thunking down again on the table.

Her eyes might have been tight shut, but Sienna could still hear the sound of a chair being drawn out and a china bowl sliding across the tabletop. The most delicious smell of cocoa, coffee, sweet liqueur and rich mascarpone wafted into her nostrils, making them twitch, and her mouth watered in anticipation of the smooth lusciousness of her favourite dessert.

'That was fast! Oh, Carla. I've really done it now, haven't I? Career over. Finished. Kaput. Perhaps I can ask my brother for a job?'

'Well, you could do that, but I have a better idea.'

Sienna flung herself backwards in the chair with shock at the sound of her favourite male voice, and almost toppled the chair over.

'Brett?'

He was wearing a superbly tailored dark suit with a beautiful pale pink check shirt and a tie the exact same shade of blue as his eyes. Her heart soared and screamed a halleluiah in joy.

She had missed him so much that just the sight of him sitting there, with his elbows on the table-cloth, smiling across at her, made her world suddenly bright.

This was why she had been so miserable for the few hours since they had been parted.

'Hello,' she whispered, trying to be brave and not embarrass herself by leaping into his arms with joy and kissing the life out of the man.

'Hello, yourself. Medals for courage under fire are in short supply at the moment, so I rescued some of my special tiramisu. I thought you might need the encouragement. It seems I need not have worried after all. Congratulations.'

'I don't deserve a medal,' she replied, lifting her head slightly to look at the bowl, heaped with delicious creamy dessert, a gold spoon leaning on the rim.

Her head lifted a little higher.

Enticing curls of dark and milk chocolate were scattered across the top of the creamy stuff in the bowl.

'Resigning from this job was a totally reckless thing to do,' she added with a sniff.

His finger slipped under her chin and lifted it higher, so that when he bent down to her level he could make direct eye contact.

'Not reckless. Right. How did you feel when you told them that you didn't want the restaurant manager's job after all?

'It felt so good!' She managed a thin smile and pushed out her lower lip before lifting her head a little more. 'Actually, it felt wonderful!' She sat bolt upright and nodded at Brett. 'You're right! It was the right thing to do! I deserve better!'

Then she remembered the flipside of that statement and groaned. 'I have been a total idiot!' She almost slumped down again, except Brett had seen it coming and propped her up by lifting up the dessert bowl and wafting it higher and higher.

'Not another word until you have given me your expert opinion on the dessert. I'm still not sure about the chocolate curls, and you know that it has to be perfect before Valentine's Day or I won't be happy.'

She reached forward and took a heaped spoonful of smooth, creamy-chocolate flavoured mascarpone and soft, soaked sponge, and the wonderful aroma hit her senses only a few seconds before she tasted the amazing dessert. Her eyes flickered in delight and sensual pleasure as each of the ingredients was savoured in turn.

'Wonderful. Absolutely wonderful. Just don't tell Chef André. He would be terribly upset.'

She replaced the spoon, before she embarrassed herself even more by scoffing the entire bowl, and felt her shoulders drop down by at least four inches.

Brett was sitting opposite her, elbows on the table and both hands under his chin. Watching her. Simply watching her. And delighting in doing so.

'Feel better?'

'Much. Thank you.' She reached out and took the hand that he was holding out to her.

'Oh, Brett. I am so disgusted with myself. I've wasted four years of my life grieving over some idealised version of a man who probably never existed in the first place. I thought all chefs were the same—you've shown me how wrong I was. When I think of all of that pain…'

She shook her head in disbelief and gave in to the tears which had formed in the corners of her eyes, swallowing down her fears and regrets.

The long, sensitive fingers tenderly smoothed the hair back from her forehead, his blue eyes flicking longingly over her face.

She sniffed before smiling back at him in thanks. 'I missed you.'

'I missed you too. You've only been gone a

few hours and Rossi's is simply not the same without you.'

She took a few calming breaths, eyes closed, before daring to look at Brett. One look. And her anger crisped, burnt, and was blown away in one sweep under the heat of that smile.

'Oh, Brett! I've made such a mess of things!'

He pretended to ignore her flushed face and puffy eyes, released her hair and took both of her hands in his before saying in a quiet and controlled voice, 'Not necessarily. Last night we talked about making choices. Well, now I have one more to offer you. What if you were in charge of *your own* business? Would that make a difference to your options?'

'What do you mean?' Sienna replied, intrigued.

'After you went to bed last night I started talking with Chris about a new idea which goes way beyond my signature restaurant. A long way!'

Brett squeezed her fingers in excitement as his eyes locked onto hers. Shining eyes, brimmed full of energy and enthusiasm.

'We want to open a chain of family restaurants. Imagine an informal but clean and well-run bistro a teenager could bring his high-school sweetheart to on their first big date. We'll run them as a franchise, based on the recipes that I come up with in my own kitchen, and with the same basic design of dining room you created this last week for Maria.'

He grinned at her with such love and fire and passion that the breath caught in her throat.

'Young couples all over Britain will have the chance to create their own version of Trattoria Rossi in their town. Good food. Informal and friendly. And not just for Valentine's Night but every other night as their family grows up. I think it would work. How about you?'

Her mouth formed a perfect oval for all of two seconds before she flung her head back and bellowed in laughter, slapping her fingers against Brett's in delight.

'It is a wonderful idea! I love it! I can't tell you how totally brilliant, brilliant and brilliant it is.'

She leant forward and kissed him, hard and quick on the lips.

'You clever man. No wonder you are excited!'

'I am. Except Chris and I have a major problem which could seriously hold the project back.'

She shrugged and pulled one hand away from his clutches to wave it in front of her face.

'Nothing that you can't handle. You're Brett Cameron! Superstar! Superhero! Tiramisu maker extraordinaire!'

'Thank you for that, but even superstars can't be in two places at the same time. I have worked all my life to open a dream restaurant in Notting Hill—and you know how that feels. It needs my total focus and dedication.'

He paused and gave her one of his special smiles before blurting out, 'I need a business partner to run our chain of family trattoria. Chris will be able to raise funding for the first year, and your aunt Maria has agreed to let me lease Rossi's from her at a special rate so that we can develop our first trattoria there, to be used as a model for the franchise—but we don't have a manager.'

Brett let that sink in for a few seconds before rushing on with his pitch. 'The ideal person would have to be used to dealing with very discerning customers, capable of running the whole business, and it would be a big help if they liked my food. And I have to be able to trust them. Completely. Know any likely candidates who might fit that description?'

Sienna froze. The smile faded on her lips.

'Are you serious? You're offering me the job?'

'No. I'm offering you a partnership in the business. You would be running *your very own* chain of family trattoria. *With* me. Not *for* me. This would be your project, using the amazing talent I've seen over these last few days. You can do this. I have no doubt about that whatsoever. You are the only person I could trust.'

'You trust me that much? You are willing to relinquish absolute control and let me make decisions without trying to interfere all the time?'

'With all my heart.'

'Wow, you know how to take the wind out of a girl's sails. I don't understand. This is *so* exciting. Why didn't you mention it before now?'

'Ah. I only came up with the idea after you had gone to bed last night, and I had to be absolutely certain of something very important before I even mentioned it. And there's the fact that you seem to like my food, of course.'

'Of course. Now talk to me. What could be that important?'

'I had to find out if you were willing to sacrifice everything to make your new job here at Greystone a success. Or not.'

Sienna sucked in a breath and stared hard at the wonderful man who had just offered her the chance to realise her dream, and something clicked into place which she had never even thought of before—and yet suddenly it made so much sense.

'Before I answer that, I do have one question for you. And it is equally important. I trust you to tell me the truth.'

She picked up the bowl of tiramisu and licked the chocolate from the spoon.

'This tiramisu wasn't just a lucky guess. Was it?'

He gave a brief shake of the head and a closed-mouth smile.

'You remembered. It was twelve years ago. But you remembered that tiramisu is my favourite dessert.'

His answer was to lift up the hand he was holding and kiss the back of her knuckles.

'Oh, Brett.'

'I was the poor boy from the wrong side of the tracks who was never going to be good enough to ask the Rossi princess out on a date. So I locked up my heart and hid the key so that it would be safe.'

His fingertip traced the curve of her eyebrow. So tenderly and lovingly it almost brought Sienna to the brink of tears again.

'So beautiful. Clever. Destined for great things. I might not have been good enough, but I paid attention.' He smiled as Sienna shook her head in disbelief. 'Your aunt Maria noticed, but kept quiet. Your dad just thought I was clumsy. I was so envious of the wonderful start in life you and Frank had. You had the family. The restaurant. You were living the kind of family life I had only dreamt about.'

Sienna groaned and pressed two fingertips to his lips.

'This might not be the best time to tell you that there was a very good reason why I stalked your every working day. Crush. I had a total girly crush on you. Only I was too shy to tell you.'

Silence.

'Not possible. If you saying that to make me feel better, I appreciate the sentiment but…'

She shrugged. 'Nope. You have the honour of having been my first crush, Brett Cameron.'

Then she grinned. 'Do you remember the other day, when I asked you to stay in the basement at the Rossi house when I went up to my old bedroom to hunt for shoes? I was *terrified* that you would come across my diary. Which includes the daily detailed itinerary of when I saw you, what you were wearing, what you said, what I did… Need I go on?'

'You…had a crush on me?'

She nodded several times, biting her lower lip, then gave up completely and started giggling, then stopped, then giggled again, then carried on giggling until he was forced to give in and roar with laughter.

'Could we have been more pathetic? You were in the kitchen, frightened to speak to me when I came in the room, while I was miserable when I wasn't in the same room as you. Both of us too shy or too scared to talk to each other. How ironic is that?'

'Crazy. I wish I'd known.'

'Me too. I do have one more question. And it's totally personal.'

'After that little bombshell I'm almost frightened to hear it, but fire away. I can handle it.'

'In that case I need to know if you are still in love with Lili. Or not.'

He stopped laughing and turned his attention to her jawline, his fingertips moving in gentle circles, then curving so that her face was being held in his hands.

'I'll never forget her, but I'm only capable of loving one woman at a time, and I'm looking at the woman I'm in love with today, and will go on loving for the rest of my life.'

Sienna looked into the depths of those amazing eyes, and what she saw there made her heart sing. Her words gushed out in joy. 'Then you will be pleased to hear that my answer is…not. A great big definite *not*.'

Brett never broke eye contact with her as he reached into his jacket pocket and pulled out a small velvet box.

Her heart was thumping so loudly in her chest that breathing and thinking and listening at the same time suddenly became a major challenge.

With the ease that suggested someone who had been practising, Brett flicked open the lid and pressed the open box into the palm of her hand.

Sienna looked down on a pink, heart-shaped solitaire diamond on an elegant platinum band, and pressed her free hand to her chest.

It was the most beautiful thing she had ever seen in her life, and she told him so.

'You're an amazing woman, Sienna Rossi. I never thought you could surprise me any more, but you have done. Any man would want to have you in his life. Want you in his bed. Make you the last thing he sees at night. The woman he wakes up with every morning.'

She knew he was smiling by the creases at the corners of his mouth.

'I was a boy who thought that he would never be good enough for someone as beautiful and clever as you. Will you give me a chance to prove that I have become a better man, who is finally worthy of you?'

'I like the man he became quite a lot. I trust him with my life—and my heart. And my dreams.'

The smile faded, his eyes darkening.

'I'm also the man who wants to hold you in his arms and have you by his side every day. I want to spend the rest of my life showing you how much I need you. How much you mean to me.'

He swept both hands down from her forehead, smoothing her hair down, over and over, building the strength to say the words. His eyes focused on hers, and his voice was broken and ragged with intensity.

'I love you, Sienna. I walked into that kitchen a lonely young man in a frightening place, terrified that he would make a mistake and mess things up, and be back on the streets. Then you turned to me and gave me a tiny shy smile.'

Her eyes glistened as he stroked her face.

'And I knew that everything was going to be okay.'

His voice broke and he could only draw her up to her full height, so that his hands could wrap around her back, pressing his body closer to hers, his head into her neck. She could sense his heaving chest as they both fought back years of suppressed desires and hopes.

She could feel the pressure of his lips on her skin, but everything was suddenly a blur. If only the fireworks would stop going off in her head. Rockets seemed to be exploding in huge ribbons of light and colour.

Brett loved her. Brett Cameron. *Loved.* Her.

With all the strength she'd thought she had lost, Sienna slid her hands from his waist up the front of his chest, resisting the temptation to rip his shirt off, and felt this man's heart thumping wildly under the cloth. His shirt was sweaty, and she could feel the moist hair under her fingers as his pulse rang out under her touch.

She forced her head back from his body, inches away from this remarkable, precious man who had exposed his deepest dreams to her.

'It broke my heart when you left for Paris. Since then I've looked everywhere for the missing part, but nobody was able to mend it. How could they, when you were simply holding it safe for me? I was just so scared that you would break it all over again. So scared.'

Her hand came up to stroke Brett's face as he looked at her in silence, his chest heaving as he forced air into his lungs. She could still hear the pounding of his heart as he spoke.

His voice was full of excitement and energy, the desire burning in every word.

'Come and work with me. Run your own business. Sleep in my arms every night.'

His eyes scanned across her face, trying to gauge her reaction.

'Will you come and live with me? Will you be my partner, my lover, and the mother of my children? Can you do that? Can you take a chance at happiness with me?'

She gasped in a breath as the tears streamed down her face, knowing that he was saying the words she had waited a lifetime to hear.

'Yes.'

He looked back at her and his mouth dropped open in shock. 'Yes?'

'Yes!' She laughed, 'Yes, yes, yes. Oh, Brett. I love you so much.'

She had barely got the words out of her mouth before she was silenced by the pressure of a pair of hot lips, which would have knocked her backwards if not for the strong arms that pressed her body to his. Eyes closed, she revelled in the glorious sensation of his mouth, lips, skin and firm body. Lights were going on in parts of her where she had not known switches existed. She felt as if she was floating on air.

Her eyes flicked open to find that she *was* floating

in air. Brett had hoisted her up by the waist, was twirling her around and around, two grown up people hooting with joy, oblivious to the tableware. A kaleidoscope of happiness, colour and light.

Sienna slid back down his body, her extended arms caressed lovingly by strong hands, looked into Brett's smiling face, stunned by the joy she had brought to this precious man, and grinned.

'Take me home, Brett. Take me home.'

CHAPTER TWENTY-TWO

Step 22: Keep Mixture Warm until Valentine's Day; Top with a Red Rose Before Serving with a Kiss

PINK FAIRY lights still twinkled and sparkled in the branches of the ornamental bay trees inside the refurbished dining room of Trattoria Rossi.

The last few days since Sienna had left Greystone Manor had passed in a blur of excitement, joy, and a lot of very hard work—but the Trattoria had finally been ready to welcome their guests on a very special Valentine's Day.

It had not only been her first Valentine's Day as the new owner of Trattoria Rossi—but the perfect engagement party, with everyone she loved around her. Even Carla had managed to escape Greystone that evening!

The last of the paying customers had gone home,

after what many had told her was the best meal of their lives. There had been Valentine kisses, holding hands under the table, and a lot of laughter and chatter. But best of all, Maria Rossi had been there in person, to help Sienna say goodbye to one part of her life and prepare to start a new one.

Sienna smiled and shook her head. The irrepressible Maria had escaped her hospital bed by promising to take it easy and recover slowly, but there was no way that lady had been going to miss her final Valentine's Day before handing the place over to Sienna and Brett.

The tables were now pushed together to create one long central eating area, with enough space around the chairs for Frankie's children to run around, laughing and playing with Jess and her new very best friends—Henry's granddaughters, who both lived in the area.

For now the room belonged to the family. *Her family.* Old and new.

It was as though every precious, warm feeling she had ever associated with her Rossi family meals had come together in one place. Now she understood how Brett had felt all those years ago.

Carla had already found a seat next to Chris, and was chatting away about the chain of Italian trattoria style bistros he was going to run for the future Mr and Mrs Cameron, while Maria took centre stage with the Rossi horde, talking of her plans to run a beach café with Henry under the Spanish sunshine.

Trattoria Rossi was still Trattoria Rossi. Only now it was Sienna's very own place. Not in competition with Brett's Notting Hill restaurant, but her own space, where she could serve wonderful food in a warm and welcoming cosy room.

This was the family restaurant she had known as a child, only better—because Brett was here. The man she loved was sitting next to her brother, Frankie, the two men flicking through one of the photo albums her mother had kept all her life, laughing as they pointed to one image then another.

Albums in which photos of her own children would be given a place once day.

Her heart expanded to take in her joy and happiness.

Palms sweaty, she gawped at the best-looking man in the room. He was wearing a chef's apron over a crisp white shirt, open at the neck, designed to highlight his deep tan and the brightness of his smile and eyes. Absolutely gorgeous.

Brett glanced over his shoulder at that moment,

and her breath caught in her throat as he returned her smile and reached out for her with a grin that made her melt and her heart soar with happiness.

Sienna bent over and kissed Brett, before leaning back and smiling at the man who had brought such joy into her life.

A single perfect red rose lay across a crystal tulip dish filled with his special recipe chocolate tiramisu.

'Happy Valentine's Day,' he whispered, his voice so full of love it took her breath away.

Today marked the end of one part of her life and the start of a lifetime of perfect Valentine's Days. With a man who knew the perfect recipe for her happiness.